Snapstreak

HOW MY FRIENDS SAVED MY ᵛsocial LIFE

Snaps

freak

BY **SUZANNE WEYN**

HOUGHTON MIFFLIN HARCOURT
BOSTON NEW YORK

WWW.HMHCO.COM

Emoji art was supplied by EmojiOne.
Styling by Lauren Litton and Lori Andrews.
The text type was set in Adobe Garamond Pro.
The display type was set in Marujo.
Patterns © Amovitania/Shutterstock (Vee, Lulu); Anya D/Shutterstock (Megan);
and Fay Francevna/Shutterstock (Gwynneth)
Book design by Sharismar Rodriguez

LIBRARY OF CONGRESS CATALOGING-IN-PUBLICATION DATA
Names: Weyn, Suzanne, author.
Title: Snapstreak : how my friends saved my (social) life / Suzanne Weyn.
Description: Boston ; New York : Houghton Mifflin Harcourt, [2018].
Summary: Told from multiple viewpoints, eighth graders Vee, Lulu, Megan,
and Gwynneth enter a local television station's contest for the pair of
students who can prove the longest-running "snapstreak."
Identifiers: LCCN 2016057655 | ISBN 9781328713469 (paper over board)
Subjects: | CYAC: Friendship—Fiction. | Social media—Fiction.
Contests—Fiction. | Middle schools—Fiction. | Schools—Fiction.
Brain—Concussion—Fiction. | Single-parent families—Fiction. | BISAC:
JUVENILE FICTION / Social Issues / Friendship. | JUVENILE FICTION /
Computers. | JUVENILE FICTION / Social Issues / Emotions & Feelings. |
JUVENILE FICTION / Sports & Recreation / General. | JUVENILE FICTION /
School & Education. | JUVENILE FICTION / General.
Classification: LCC PZ7.W539 Snd 2018 | DDC [Fic]—dc23
LC record available at https://lccn.loc.gov/2016057655

Manufactured in China
SCP 10 9 8 7 6 5 4 3 2 1
4500682844

For Diana Weyn Gonzalez
and Rae Weyn Gonzalez: love always.

Snapstreak

CHAPTER 1

NOW THAT PLAN A has bombed—Dad covered his ears last night when I begged him not to move us to Shoreham—I need a plan B.

Blackmail? ("I saw you steal the neighbor's paper, Dad. I don't care if they're on vacation! Promise we won't move or I'm telling them.")

Taking our dachshund hostage? ("You had better promise not to leave this house if you ever want to see Heidi Dog again.")

Pretending to have amnesia? ("Are you my dad? I don't know. The only thing I remember is this house. This house. Which. I. Can. Never. Leave.") I've never actually met anyone with amnesia but I think it's a really cool idea.

It would be so freaky to not remember who you are or your past life. Secretly, I'd like to try it sometime. Not forever, of course—just a couple of days of temporary amnesia to see what it's like.

I might as well get real—none of these ideas is going to work. I'm just going to have to accept that Dad and I and Eric (my pest brother) will be moving to a brand-new town when I start high school. The move will put Dad closer to his new job. It doesn't matter that the town is only ten miles away. It might as well be a hundred miles! Kids who live in Pleasant Hill don't hang with kids from Shoreham. It's just too far away. It's as if I'm moving to another country—another planet.

I don't want to be the new kid. I'll be shunned! An outsider! An outcast wandering the halls of Shoreham High School like the invisible ghost of the formerly cheery, friendly, and—to be honest—fashionable girl I used to be. No one will even realize I'm there. That's how it is with new kids. Even if you smile at them and wave and try to be helpful, they know they don't really fit in. Everybody knows it. And now that tragic figure is going to be ME!

But wait.

Maybe not!

Something unbelievable just happened.

My phone buzzed. I thought it would be Megan or Lulu. But it isn't!

It's Gwynneth!

My heart is racing.

How did she even find me?

Oh yeah—I wrote my username on her palm, but still . . .

Feeling like a mermaid on OBX

I can't believe she contacted me. Getting a Snap from Gwynneth is beyond awesome.

Listen to this: Last week I was standing in front of my new home-to-be while Dad talked to the real estate lady. I was just staring at the house. (More like glaring at it, willing the house to explode.) A tall girl wearing lots of bangles and heavy eyeliner strolled up to me along with three of her BFFs. This girl was clearly the Queen Bee with her three Wanna-Bees hovering. She shot me the once-over with her narrowed, black-rimmed eyes. "You moving into Emma's old place?" she asked.

Leaning onto one hip, I folded my arms. "Maybe, who's asking?"

The corner of her mouth twitched into an approving grin. Her teeth glistened with spit from the gum she chomped. "Gwynneth, that's who."

"Hi, G.," I said. "I'm Vee."

The Wanna-Bees erupted into a buzz of chuckles.

"V for victory?" Gwynneth asked.

My name is really Olivia, but when Eric was a baby, all he could say was Vee, and it stuck. I wasn't going to tell them all that, though. "Maybe" is all I said.

Gwynneth raised a fist and I bumped it. "Welcome to the nabe, Vee," she said in a turn to friendliness. Taking a short, stubby eyeliner from her pocket, she grabbed my palm and wrote on it: *GQB2the2ndpwr.* "If you need help finding your way around, Snapchat me," she said.

One of her Bee drones stepped forward and poked the writing on my palm. "Gwynneth is really awesome at math," she informed me with a knowing nod.

"Excellent," I replied, making sure not to seem too impressed. I took her hand and her eyeliner and wrote *V-Ness.* "That's me."

"Venus, the goddess of love," Gwynneth said, nodding with approval. She flashed a thumbs-up as she and her pals continued on their way. "See ya," Gwynneth said.

"See ya," I said.

Gwynneth could be the lifesaver I need. If I get in good with her now, then I'll have a pal when I get to Shoreham High. I'll be in with the in-crowd. Genius! (Don't mind my bragging—but it's an awesome plan.) Only, I felt funny about it. There's a part of me that's shy with new people. I'd put off contacting Gwynneth because I didn't know what to say.

But now here she is. Gwynneth has contacted me!

I stare at my phone. What could I say that would sound cool? Not needy or nervous. Before I can think of anything, my phone buzzes. It's one of my main girls, Lulu. I always smile when I see her username, Luloony, because it's very *her*. She can be sort of zany and loopy, but in a fun way. She's probably responding to the Snap I sent to her and Megan earlier.

Luloony

Wanna hang later?

V-Ness

👍

Luloony

What did you think of my Snap??

V-Ness

The flower crown? So pretty!

V-Ness

Wud it b cool to use that filter with someone
I want to impress?

Luloony

Yeah! Who?

V-Ness

GQB2the2ndpwr

Luloony

?

Luloony

V-Ness

Luloony

Why?????

V-Ness

I'm going to need friends in Shoreham . . .

🩶🏫

Talk to you later. Dad's taking me shopping at the mall.

Luloony

What are you getting?

V-Ness

Need new sneaks.
I want a new pair of Chucks. High-tops, I think.

Luloony

Cool. Send a Snap!

V-Ness

Did you hear the new Boys Being Dudes song?

Luloony

No. Is it good?

V-Ness

Really good! You should check it out.

Luloony

LOVE them!

Luloony

V-Ness

You will 🖤

Luloony

Thnx!

V-Ness

Omg! Gwynneth is snapping me.
OMG!!!!!!!!!!!!!!!!!!!!!!!!!!!!!!

CHAPTER 2

VEE CAN BE so annoying. Like at this very moment. She knows I'm freaked out that she's moving. But clearly she's moved on already.

Moooved on! So long, Lulu! It's been real but I already have a new BFF.

As if Gwynneth is now her everything.

Guh-win-ith! What a name, huh? What kind of person is named Gwynneth, anyway?

And not only THAT!!!!

Not only is Vee on her way to forgetting her former friends—she wants ME to help replace myself.

I feel bad about saying this, but I was happier when

she was crying all the time about having to move. (And I mean ALL the time. On the school bus. In the cafeteria. During gym.) At least then I knew Vee was heartbroken to be leaving Megan and me. At least then it was clear how much she was going to miss us.

And it was a lot.

I felt a sad kind of happy.

But now she's all tra-la-la . . . moving along.

I need to vent.

I'm texting Megan.

Wait, no! Megan's messaging me! (Great minds, and all that.)

Megawatt

Hey! What's up? 🩶

Luloony

Gwynnwitch. 😡

Megawatt

?????

Luloony

Vee wants to be friends with G!

Megawatt

Okay. SO?

Luloony

Noooooooooooooooooooooooooooo!!!!!!!

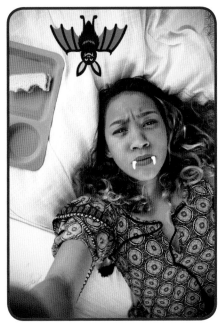

Megawatt

She'll need some friends.

Luloony

She only needs us!!!!!

Megawatt

Why not us plus G?

Luloony

No. We are the only friends she needs.

🤍 🤍 🤍

Megawatt

Vee will be lonely, though.

Luloony

We'll see her!

Megawatt

How?

Luloony

🚙

Megawatt

We can't drive.

Luloony

🚲

Megawatt

Too far

Luloony

Megawatt

Sorry. Don't worry so much.

Luloony
I'll try.
Hey, have you heard the new BBD tune? It dropped this morning.

Megawatt

No! Not yet. I 🖤 Joe, the drummer.

Luloony

> For reals? No one likes him. Derek is way cuter and cooler. And those Pokémon T-shirts he wears are so goofy.

Megawatt

Luloony

> Whatevs. Ttyl.

Megawatt

> Bye

So here's the thing that Megan doesn't get. I don't make friends that easily. Megan and Vee have other friends. I don't. They're my friends. That's it.

I'm not exactly sure why this is. My mom says I'm too fussy about people. She says I'm a fault finder. But I don't go searching for people's faults. They're pretty much right out there. And it's not like I don't have any faults. I have plenty: I'm hypercritical (as I just said); I can't resist gooey desserts; I get bored really easily; and sometimes (always) I speak before I think. Mom says I'm like my dad in that way. (Could that be one of the reasons they got divorced—because Dad would talk without thinking? Maybe I'd better try to be more careful about that.)

I have good qualities too, but not everyone appreciates them and that can be a drag. Recently I took a chunk of my dark hair and turned it into rainbow hair. It wasn't easy because I had to strip the dark color away with peroxide and then lay in five different colors. It took forever! I thought the kids at school would love it, but I got a lot of stares and not many compliments.

Vee, of course, adores my mermaid hair. "It's so fashion forward," she said. I told her that it didn't seem to be a big hit and she just laughed. "Not everyone is as cool and creative as you are," she said. "Who cares what they like? It's so YOU."

"But is that a good thing?" I asked.

Vee cracked up at that, laughing so hard tears ran down her cheeks. "Of course it's a good thing. It's a great thing! There's lots of them but only one you."

So as you can see, Vee is not the kind of friend I want to lose.

My only other friend is Megan. I don't want to lose her either. Even though she's not moving away, without Vee to connect us, Megan and I could drift.

It wouldn't be something we'd want to happen. It just kind of would. When you're in a group of three friends, one of the friends is always the link that keeps the threesome connected. In our case, Vee is the glue. Without Vee, Megan and I don't have enough in common to stick together. Megan already has a bunch of other friends. I just know she'd drift in their direction until all that was left of our friendship would be a smile and a wave as we passed in the hallway.

Though Megan does unexpected stuff sometimes. Like loving Joe, the drummer from BBD. I didn't even know she likes their music. She usually likes grunge rock. I think she got into it from her older sister, Paula. Paula and Megan both have that same flannel shirt, jeans, and Vans look. It doesn't look bad, but, you know, it's a LOOK. And liking a certain kind of music goes with it. BBD is completely pop. Not at all Megan's style. She must be super crushing on this Joe guy. It's the only thing that explains it.

So Megan is kind of a mystery in ways. Like, she's always writing something that she refuses to show us. She guards it like she works for the CIA and she's writing secret spy instructions. (Could that be it?!)

Anyway, without Vee and Megan I'll be the lonely girl with the mermaid hair who sits by herself at lunch and is the last one picked on every volleyball team in gym. Speaking of gym (not my favorite activity at ALL), tomorrow is lacrosse. Vee is a great player. She'll be a captain and will pick Megan and me to be on her team, sparing us the humiliation of being last called. (No other captains in their right minds would want us. They've seen us play. It's not a pretty picture.)

My phone buzzes like crazy. I have five new Snaps, all from Vee. Five pictures of five different pairs of shoes.

Megan must have gotten the same Snap.

Megan: The black ones.

Lulu: Definitely the gold.

Vee: I'll ask G. Bye!

I'm stunned! No, I'm mad! No, I'm hurt. I don't know! I'm all those things. Ask G? Ask G?!

Lulu: Do you believe her?

Megan: What?

Lulu: Vee!!!!! She's going to ask G??????????????????

Megan: No biggie. Mom's calling me for supper.

Lulu: Kk. Ltr.

It's happening already. Vee is off with G and Megan is losing patience with me. I know she doesn't want to hear me complain. Note to self: Stop complaining so much. What is going to happen to me if I have no friends? It's such a disaster I can't even stand to think about it.

I hear Mom come in the front door so I slide off my bed and go to say hi. At the top of the stairs I see she's staggering under the weight of two grocery bags, so I hurry down to take one from her. "How was your day?" she asks.

I sigh deeply. "Just the usual mix of betrayal and confusion," I say, thinking of Vee.

Mom puts her bag on the counter and turns to me, alarmed. "What happened?"

"It's only life, Mom. You should know what it's like by now. My best friends have abandoned me, that's all."

"Lulu, what's going on?"

Settling my bag on the table, I wilt into a chair. "I'm about to enter the barren desert of the friendless. No biggie! I'll be fine. NOT!"

"Is this because Vee is moving?"

"Yes, and Megan is distancing herself emotionally, too."

Mom starts unpacking the groceries. "Lulu, I think

you're making too much of this. Those girls will always be your friends, no matter what."

"Will they?" I ask, letting my head drop into my arms.

"Who knows? Only time will tell." Mom believes this is nothing to worry about. She has no idea how deeply the idea of losing my two friends torments me.

CHAPTER 3

LULU MAKES SUCH a big deal over things. A huge deal. She's an artistic type and that's how artistic types act, I guess. DRAMATIC! DRAMATIC! DRAMATIC!

Sure, I'm going to miss Vee, too. The three of us are like sisters. Vee's mother died when we were in sixth grade, and we totally surrounded her because she was an absolute mess. Lulu and I never let Vee be alone; we called and texted her day and night. Not that being a mess wasn't perfectly understandable. It was her mother, after all. We just wanted to be there for Vee whenever she might need us.

All the shared emotion and togetherness made the three of us tight. There's no doubt about that. We're pretty much as close as three friends can be.

I'm just more realistic than Lulu. People move all the time. It doesn't mean Vee is going to disappear. We're too tight for that.

Lulu isn't the only one who is completely freaked about Vee. I care too. I'm just trying to make the best of it. You know, figure out ways we can stay connected. People around the world form friendships and stay connected. We'll always have Snapchat! Moving one town over shouldn't be a deal breaker. But Lulu can be a total Eeyore sometimes. It's frustrating when she refuses to stay positive. I believe that staying positive is something a person must, must, must do. (Naturally, a person has to also be a realist. We won't see Vee as much and she'll make new friends other than us. I just think we have too much history and love for it all to go away because of distance.)

My phone is buzzing. It's a Snap from Lulu. This is what she sends me:

Luloony

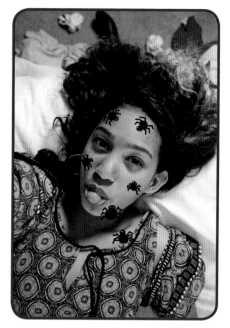

Megawatt

V nice!

Luloony

I take a video of my room and close in on my cat, Wags. I add a filter so that Wags pukes a rainbow. I send it to Vee and Lulu.

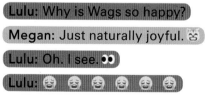

Lulu: Why is Wags so happy?

Megan: Just naturally joyful. 😸

Lulu: Oh. I see. 👀

Lulu: 😩 😩 😩 😩 😩 😩

Megan: Why so sad?

Vee: What you feeding Wags, Meggie?

Vee: Hey! LX Thursday. ☺

Lulu: For reals? Are you crazy? I hate lacrosse.

Lulu: I hope it rains. ⚡🌧️☂️

Vee: I want to show off my new sneaks. 👟

Megan: Show us!

Vee: Like?

Lulu: G pick these?

Vee: Thanks! No. Didn't have the nerve to ask her.

Vee: What would be cool for me to send to Gwynneth?

Megan: Puke a rainbow. 🌈

Vee: Come on, guys! Think! 😐

Lulu: 🙈

Vee: Come onnnnnn!!! I don't want her to think I'm ignoring her. If we start chatting maybe I can meet her other friends. Then I'll know some kids when I get to Shoreham.

Lulu: You're not GOING to Shoreham.

Vee: I am. 😤

Lulu: We'll figure something out. I'll ask Mom if you can live with me!

Vee: Yeah?

Lulu: I'll ask.

Vee: ☺ ☺ ☺ ☺ ☺ ☺

Megan: See you tomorrow.

I have to get off that group text before I go crazy, crazy, crazy. Lulu and Vee are out of their minds if they think Vee's dad would ever let her live with Lulu, even on the one-in-a-bazillion chance that Lulu's mother agrees to it. Lulu and Vee can be kind of delusional sometimes—like the time they entered a contest so we could go to Hollywood and appear as extras in a movie. They figured one of them would win and then sneak the other two onto the set. I'm telling you, they were planning what to pack and what they'd say to all the stars they met. Maybe it was just for fun, but they sure acted like they thought they really were going to Hollywood.

I'm the sensible one of the three of us. Vee and Lulu always say so. But does that mean I'm boring?

I don't think so. In my head there's lots going on. I LOVE to read and from there I spin the story out for miles. Bilbo Baggins from *The Hobbit* is my favorite character and I write fan fiction about him, giving him fun new adventures out of the Shire. I even make up new enemies for Bilbo to outwit. Last week I made up a creature who is half beast and half witch. She's based on our gym teacher, Ms. Pate. There's an online site where I post my fan fiction. But no one can see my writing except other fans who go to that site.

Lulu and Vee never see my fan fiction. I'm too shy to show them. I know they wouldn't be mean to my face. They'd say it was good. At least, I think it's good. Since they're my best friends, I should be able to show it to them, shouldn't I? I don't really know why I can't. Maybe someday I will.

CHAPTER 4

THIS MORNING I send Gwynneth a picture of my new sneakers.

Lame?

I know!

I can't think of anything else and I'm desperate! I'm sitting on my bed wishing I could take it back. Sneakers! Of all the dumb things! What if she hates these sneakers, thinks they're too . . . too much. The kids at school expect me to be a fashionista, always a little bit out there with my styles. Part of my VEEness is being V-Ness. A little flash! A little dash! That's me. But what if Gwynneth just thinks the sneakers are low class? Too flashy? (I think they're known to be kind of rich-kid posh over in Shoreham.)

Or maybe—even worse—what if she thinks it's juvenile to send a photo of sneakers? Maybe it IS babyish! Am I juvenile? No! Deep breath. Of course I'm not. No more juvenile than any other kid in my eighth grade, anyway. (We have some real toddler types, mostly some of the boys. OMG! What if I'm like them? No. Definitely not.)

My phone buzzes and I see the baby icon by the notification.

I haven't seen that in a while. A new friend is Snapping me.

A NEW friend!

She's a new friend. A FRIEND!!!! She wants to be my friend!

OMG.

Gwynneth!

I hope.

Yes!!!

OMG! OMG!

I'd better see what she's sent. My hands are actually trembling.

GQB2the2ndpwr

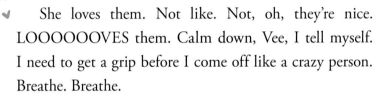

She loves them. Not like. Not, oh, they're nice. LOOOOOOVES them. Calm down, Vee, I tell myself. I need to get a grip before I come off like a crazy person. Breathe. Breathe.

V-Ness

Needed new sneakers for gym tomorrow

GQB2the2ndpwr

No way. Save them for good. Gym will wreck them.

V-Ness

You're probably right.

GQB2the2ndpwr

V-Ness

Lol! Thnx.

GQB2the2ndpwr

Gotta go. Don't wreck the sneaks.

I sit on the bus with my new sneakers in a plastic yellow grocery bag. "Why aren't you wearing the new ones?" Lulu asks as she slides into the seat beside me and checks out my old ripped red Cons.

"I sent a Snap of them to Gwynneth and she thought they were so awesome that I shouldn't ruin them in gym."

"Well, I guess Gwynneth knows all," Lulu says sourly. "Did you send her the same shot you sent us?"

"No, a better one."

"Why did you send her a better one?" Lulu is SO sensitive! I could tell right away by the look in her eyes that I'd hurt her feelings.

"It wasn't really better," I say, "it was . . . a different angle, and I was posing in them. That's all."

Lulu humphs. "If you're saving your sneakers then why are they in a bag?"

"Because gym is first period. I'm going to put them on after gym."

"Was that Gwynneth's brilliant idea?"

"No. Mine."

"That will certainly preserve their golden sparkle," Lulu says. I hate when she gets like this, all snarky and sarcastic. I know her so well. She's all snide when her feelings are hurt. I should never have told her I sent Gwynneth a better picture of my sneakers. The whole thing is super dumb, but for Lulu it's a matter of life and death.

"So? Did you ask your mom about me living with you?" I ask this partly to get off the sore subject of sneaker Snaps. Also, though, I want to know.

Last night I had a hard time falling asleep. I lay awake wondering what Shoreham High would be like. I've been there twice. One time was to see a school production of

The Wizard of Oz. (Their school is known for their almost-professional plays.) The second time I went there to see a basketball game. Shoreham High is a shiny, spiffy, new-ish school. It's not like Pleasant Hill High School, which has been around since 1952 and is all scuffy and dull. Shoreham High kind of gleams. I pictured myself as one of Gwynneth's Wanna-Bees, which wasn't exactly a great image, even if I got to be the number one Wanna-Bee. But the pathetic-new-kid image was even worse.

Then I pictured living with Lulu . . .

Don't get me wrong, I love Lulu. I'm not sure I love Lulu enough to actually live with her, though. For one thing, Lulu's room looks like a trailer park after a tornado blew through. I once got a peanut butter and jelly sandwich stuck to the bottom of my shoe in there. Last week, I saw her pull an overdue library book she borrowed in third grade from a pile of clothing that was as tall as she is. There is no extra room in Lulu's house, so that's the room I'd be sharing with her.

"Mom says she'll think about it," Lulu replies. "What did your dad say?"

"I didn't ask. No sense getting him all worked up until your mom agrees."

"Do you think he'll freak out?"

"At first," I say.

Lulu nods but says nothing. She's a great friend and

maybe it would be fun to live with her. I'd miss Dad and even Eric, not to mention Heidi Dog.

Would living with Lulu be better than being a Gwynneth Wanna-Bee, or the lone pathetic kid at Shoreham High? I don't know. It's very confusing. Thinking about it makes my head hurt.

Megan gets on the bus at the next stop. As soon as she takes a seat in front of Lulu and me, her face twists into a deep yawn. "Sorry," she says. "I was up late last night writing."

"Writing what?" Lulu asks.

Megan's eyes go wide and her mouth tightens. "Nothing!" she says in a squeak.

"How can you write nothing?" I ask.

"Emails," she says. "Emails to my cousins."

"What cousins?" Lulu says. "I never heard of you having cousins."

"I have some. In Australia. My cousins in Australia."

Lulu's eyes narrow suspiciously. "What are their names?"

"Uh, Barbie. And Bindi. They're second cousins, really. Maybe even third or fourth cousins."

"Barbie and Bindi, huh?" Lulu rolls her eyes. I try not to laugh. It's so obviously a lie. Megan has never, ever mentioned Barbie and Bindi before.

"You'd love them," Megan adds.

"I'm sure I would," Lulu says. She shakes her head and throws me a LOOK that asks, what's up with her? I reply with a quick shrug. Sometimes Megan becomes all mysterious, like she's hiding something, almost as if she's some kind of undercover agent with a secret life. I have no idea what's behind all the secrecy.

"Anyway, you must be happy, Lulu," Megan says. "Look at the sky."

Lulu and I gaze up at the mass of grayness with its rolling black clouds. It hadn't been that overcast when I got on the bus. Two fat, wet splotches smack onto the window.

"No outdoor lacrosse today," Megan says.

"Finally, something's going right," Lulu says with a smile.

By the time we get off the bus, it is pouring rain. The hallway is a muddy, squishy trail of dripping kids. It doesn't take long to hurry from the bus to the front door of school, but it was enough to soak all of us.

At the locker next to mine, Megan tosses her hair back and sprays me like a wet dog shaking its fur. "Hey! Cut it out!" I shout.

"Oh, sorry," Megan says with a giggle.

I stuff my grocery bag of new sneakers into the top of my locker. There's no way I'm wearing them today in the murky, damp halls. "Oh snap!" Megan cries. "I just remembered we had homework in pre-algebra."

"Do it in the gym," I say. "We'll probably get a skills period. You know it always happens when it rains."

"I hope so," Megan says, pulling her pre-algebra workbook from her locker shelf.

Lulu comes around the corner and we head toward the gym. It's odd when gym is first period because we have to listen to the morning announcements, take attendance, and salute the flag with a double class of forty or so girls. It takes forever. Sometimes the boys have gym with us and other times they're separated by a movable wall.

Today the wall is up, for which I am very happy. It means I won't have to spend the entire gym period trying not to look at Ethan Myers. (Ethan Myers, with the most adorable big brown eyes and shaggy, brown hair. He wears the coolest T-shirts from all the rock concerts he's been to. Plus he's at least two inches taller than most of the others guys, maybe even three.) We're neighbors, but he doesn't pay much attention to me . . . until the last couple of weeks, that is. Suddenly he's always smiling and waving to me. He has definitely noticed me. It's so exciting.

I'm sitting cross-legged on the gym floor when my phone buzzes. A text from Lulu, who is sitting way across the room, since we have to arrange ourselves in alphabetical order:

Lulu: Be cool and turn sloooowly to the door. EM alert.

EM? I don't get it at first—and then I do.

Ethan Myers is peeking around the wall! He smiles at me! Is he looking for me? Me?

"MYERS!" A deep male voice bellows from the other side. It's Mr. Green, the boys' phys ed teacher. Ethan ducks his head back and disappears.

I start to text Lulu back: "Omg! I can't belie—"

I stop short because I'm suddenly staring at a pair of bare legs topped by gym shorts. Gazing up, I stare into Ms. Pate's angry eyes. "How many times have we talked about leaving the cell phone in your locker, Vee?" my gym teacher asks. (It's kind of a snarl, more than an ask.) She has a strict "no cell phones" policy.

"I'll put it away," I say. "No problem."

"Yes, problem," Ms. Pate says. "Give me that phone."

I hand it to her and she reads my texts to Lulu. It occurs to me that it's a violation of my privacy, but it also occurs to me that it would be best not to argue with her at this moment. As she reads, my phone buzzes again. I cringe. Who could it be?

Ms. Pate stares down at me. "Megan wants you to know that EM was just looking in here for you. He's dreamy and def hearts you," Ms. Pate reads. Nearby some girls giggle. This is so humiliating!

Ms. Pate scans the sea of heads in the room. "Lulu Vance and Megan Hardwick, please come here." Lulu and Megan cross the gym to join me and Ms. Pate. "Girls, I'm sick of talking to you about this. Get to the SAP room now," Ms. Pate says.

SAP stands for student academic probation. Detention. Spend too much time in SAP—more than three visits is too much—and you're suspended.

For even one SAP, a call home is made, and a letter is sent. It isn't good.

For me this is SAP one.

Then something amazing happens.

CHAPTER 5

I'M SORT OF liking being in SAP. It's a new experience. And it's not gym. I'm enjoying the book we have to read in ELA, *The Witch of Blackbird Pond,* so I don't mind sitting here reading it. I'm having fun imagining that I am the witch, imprisoned in this dungeon with two other witches, and that the teacher is my jailer.

Megan is finishing her homework, scribbling in her pre-algebra workbook like a speed demon. So the SAP thing is working for her.

But Vee not so much. She's got a pencil between two fingers that she is flipping up and down very fast. Her right foot is jiggling, too. I'm dying to text her and ask why she's so jittery, but Ms. Pate has my phone. All our phones.

It's kind of freaky to have Ms. Pate holding my phone. I feel so vulnerable. What if a meteor crashes into the school and it catches fire? I can't call Mom to come get me. Plus all my pictures and texts and stuff are there—not that there's anything so terrible, but still . . . It's MY stuff. I knew I should have set a passcode, but it always seemed like a pain. I don't like the feeling that right now Ms. Pate could be looking at the Snapchat videos I've saved. (My favorite is the one where Vee and I are changed into ants and our voices are altered to sound high and squeaky. I say, "I'm an ant. I'm very antsy." It's hilarious.)

I sit there trying to remember everything that's in my phone in case there's something there that I'm going to have to explain. (Like why I have the Joke-of-the-Hour phone line in my favorite contacts and call it every hour, even though I'm not supposed to have my phone with me. That could be a problem.)

Suddenly I wonder—have I fallen asleep? I ask myself this because I seem to be in a dream. In this dream, the newscaster from Channel 14 walks into the room and smiles at all of us. Vee stands up abruptly, her pencil dropping to the floor, and shouts, "Heather May! How is this happening? Is it really you?"

"What?! What?!" Megan squeaks, snapped out of her math haze by the sound of Vee's voice. "What's happening?" Then she sees Heather May and gives a little yelp, almost like a small dog yipping with fright.

It's dawning on me that I am NOT dreaming and Heather May from Channel 14 News is, in fact, standing in our dreary little SAP prison looking much shorter and thinner than she appears on TV and dripping rain from the hem of her expensive-looking trench coat. The teacher stands, looking surprised and shaken, too. "You're Heather May!" she says.

Heather May beams her wide TV smile on us and her perfect teeth shine. "Is this the SAP room?" she asks. "I was told to report here."

"Why, are you being punished?" Vee asks.

Heather May laughs and steps farther into the room. Pulling off her wet trench, she sits in a desk and brushes back her damp blond hair with her perfectly manicured fingers. "I need to interview some real-life teens," she tells us, "so I phoned the school and asked if I could come down. Your principal didn't want me to disturb classes but said I could interview anyone who was in the SAP room."

"Oh, sure," I say. "It's okay to disturb us, as if we don't matter." I'm not truly offended, but it's the principle of the thing.

"You're under no obligation to talk to me," Heather May says.

"Don't mind her. Will we be on TV?" Vee asks.

"My cameraperson will be joining us in a moment if that's all right. Anyone who doesn't want to be on camera needn't be."

"I don't needn't," I say, immediately feeling foolish. "I mean, there's no reason why I can't be on camera." Who doesn't want to be on TV?! You're practically not even real unless you've been on TV. (Okay, that might be a little extreme. I admit it. Still, being on camera viewed by lots of people means you really exist. Maybe that's why they call it reality TV. I don't know. Maybe not. I'm still working on this theory. Anyway, I was excited about maybe appearing on TV.)

Ms. Pate appears at the SAP room door with our phones in her hands. She puts them on the teacher's desk. "They said in the office that you might need these," she says.

"Awesome!" Megan cries, grabbing her phone from the desk. "Thanks!"

"Keep that turned off and in your locker," Ms. Pate says as she leaves.

"My special report is going to be on the effect of social media on today's teens," Heather May tells us.

My mom is always watching the part of Channel 14 News where it says, "Heather May with a special report." She's going to flip when she sees me on TV.

A woman dressed all in black with long dark hair in a braid enters the SAP room. She mounts a camera on a tripod and looks through it. "I need you girls to cluster around Heather. Squeeze in tight so I can get you all in the shot."

This is really happening!

After taking the shot, we all sit back down in a semi-circle around Heather May. She asks us a lot of questions about how we use social media: how often; which apps; how many hours a day. "Is a product more appealing to you if a lot of people like it?" she asks.

"Hmm . . . I never thought of that," Vee says. The way she says it makes me laugh. She tilts her head and puts her finger up to her chin. Very actor-like. "I don't think so," Vee continues. "I'm very much my own person and not affected by my peers."

It's too much! I let out a loud *HA*.

"What?" Vee asks, scowling at me. "It's true!"

"You don't care what a certain Gwynneth thinks of you?" I say.

A look of panic comes onto Vee's face. "Is this going to be on TV?"

"I stopped the camera," the woman in black says.

"Good," Vee says. "You know, if I'm going to be on TV I should get my new sneakers." She looks to the teacher. "Can I go to my locker for a sec?"

The teacher says it's fine. While Vee is gone, Megan and I tell Heather May how much we love Snapchat and how it's our main app for communicating. We show her some of the funny filters: the one where our faces collapse; my favorite, where a person seems to spit up the ocean; the one where your face turns into a dog. She cracked up!

When Vee returns a few minutes later all of us, even the teacher, are laughing really hard.

"Have any of you ever been involved in a Snapstreak?" Heather May asks us as the camerawoman clicks on the video once more. "It came up in my research."

"Not intentionally," Megan says. "But we Snap each other so much that sometimes it just sort of happens. That little fire icon pops up and the number next to it tells you how many days you've been Snapping back and forth without a break."

"I've seen that," I say. "When the hourglass icon pops up, it means that you have only four hours left before twenty-four hours is up. If you go more than twenty-four hours between Snaps, you've broken the Snapstreak."

"If you did pay attention—you know, focus on it—do you think you could keep a streak going?" Heather May asks.

We look at each other with questioning eyes. Could we? "I guess," Megan says. "I don't think it would be all that hard. You have twenty-four hours to do it."

"Sometimes I run out of battery," I add.

"Do you mean you're not always paying attention to your phone?" Heather May asks.

Again we look at each other uncertainly. "Not aaal-waays," I say. "We have to sleep. And you can't really take it into the shower unless you have a waterproof case."

"I have a waterproof case," Megan says. "It's pretty

hard to use with wet hands, but you could just read it and not type."

"So are you girls saying that you're always aware of your phones except when you're sleeping?" Heather May asks.

"Sometimes I wake up in the middle of the night and can't fall back to sleep," Vee says. "I check my phone then."

"Maybe that's why you can't get back to sleep," Heather May says.

"You might be right," Vee says. "I want to go back to sleep but I'm curious to see if someone's posted on Instagram or sent me a message or a Snap."

"So you'd say social media interferes with your sleep?" Heather May asks.

"I guess it does," Vee replies.

"Does it interfere with schoolwork?"

This time the three of us look at each other because we realize this is a tricky question. The quickest way to ensure that our parents will take away our phones is to admit—on TV—that we are paying more attention to our phones than to our schoolwork. We're not falling for that! "Oh noooooooooo," I say. "School comes before phone."

"Yes, it does! Always!" Vee says, speaking at the same time as me.

"School first! Always!" Megan says at the same time Vee speaks.

"At the front office they told me you girls were in here

because you were texting during gym," Heather May says.

Silence. Why did they have to go tell her that?

"Well . . . " Vee begins as she squirms in her seat. "It was a very important matter. It couldn't wait."

"Isn't it school policy that you're not allowed to use your phones during classes?" Heather May asks.

More silence.

"It was gym," Megan says.

"Isn't physical education a required class?" Heather May asks.

Megan pushes some hair behind her ear and I can see her lobes are reddening with embarrassment. "Technically . . . yes . . . but . . ."

Heather May's eyes brighten merrily. "It's okay," she says with a chuckle. "I don't mean to put you girls on the spot. I'm getting the picture. Your phones are a huge part of your lives."

"That's it!" Vee says. "You got it!"

"Excellent, girls," Heather May says, getting up from the desk where she'd been seated. Then she remembers something. "One last question: What kind of music do you girls like?"

"All different kinds," I say.

"If you could go to a concert right now, who would you like to see?" she asks.

"BOYS BEING DUDES!" the three of us answer at the same time.

Heather May and her camerawoman both laugh. "That was pretty definite," Heather May says.

"Joe, the drummer, is really cute," Megan tells her. "And you just know from looking at him that he's a nice guy."

"No way," Vee says. "Lulu and I are both stuck on Derek, the lead singer. But Lulu is in for a disappointment because he's mine."

"That's what you think?" I say.

"Aren't those guys too old for you?" the camerawoman asks.

"No way!" Vee replies. "Derek is nineteen. I'm almost fourteen. That's nothing, especially as you get older. He'll wait for me."

"You mean he'll wait for me," I say.

"We'll see," Vee says. Of course, we know this is all imaginary. But a girl can dream, can't she? Derek has these gorgeous dark eyes. When you see the group perform it's as if he's looking right at you. I don't know how he does it, seeming to sing to you and no one else. I can't imagine what Megan sees in Joe. He's not the least bit as cool as Derek. I guess it takes all kinds—or whatever it is they say. There's no accounting for taste. They say that, too. Whatevs.

"When will this be on?" Vee asks.

"In two days, at the end of our regular show. Tune in around seven fifteen." She gives us some releases our parents have to sign saying we have their permission to be on TV. "You can fax them, scan and send electronically, or even drive them down to the studio. The address is on the form."

"Can we get a picture with you?" Vee asks Heather May. We gather around and the camerawoman takes the picture. "And can I have one with just me?" Vee asks. Heather May agrees.

"Now I have something really cool to Snap to Gwynneth," Vee says, smiling so hard it looks like her face will crack.

Gwynneth again!

CHAPTER 6

MEGAN

LATE THAT NIGHT, I take one last Snap.

I add the JK and the emoji at the last minute before I post the Snap. I don't want anyone to think I actually think I'm a star.

Sleep is impossible because I keep picturing myself on TV. I hope my hair is okay and that I don't sound dumb. A lot of times I hate the way my voice sounds when I hear it on videos. When I hear my own voice in real life, it sounds all right. On videos though, it's so much higher! What if I sound horrible on TV? I regret that Snap. I should have sent a Snap telling them to watch something else at that time. That way no one would hear my horrible high-pitched whistle of a voice.

I take a new Snap.

JK! Nothing on
Channel 14 News Saturday.

Looking down at my phone screen, I change my mind. That's just too nuts. I delete it. Maybe my voice isn't as bad as I think. I hope not.

I put in my headphones and listen to the new BBD song "New Girl in My 🖤." Great title! Normally BBD would be way too pop for me, but there's something about the BBD sound that I like a lot. Maybe it's the drum solo in every song.

Listening to music usually calms me but it's not doing the trick tonight. I have this waking dream that makes me sit up straight in my bed. In it, Joe is home watching TV. At first when he sees me on Channel 14 News he thinks: "Who's that cute girl?" Then, the moment I open my mouth, he cringes and clicks off the TV, his ears still throbbing with pain. What an awful voice, he thinks. Horrible! Horrible! Horrible!

I write some fan fiction to calm myself. Bilbo Baggins journeys away from the Shire in search of his true voice. He believes that the high, squeaky voice he currently has belongs to an evil elf. The elf took Bilbo's Hobbit voice. His friend Sam meets him along the way and tells Bilbo that he's wrong. He's always sounded like that. But Bilbo continues on, determined that this awful voice can't really be his own.

The next morning the first thing I do when I wake up is check my phone. Over forty kids want to know what's happening on Saturday. It's amazing the number of people who respond to your posts during the night and the early hours in the morning. Reading through them, I smile. Some just sent a golden trophy emoji like the Oscar.

Seven o'clock, time to get going to school. They say things look better in the morning and I guess it's true. I no longer have the jitters about my voice. I can't sound THAT bad, can I? Getting out of bed, I toss my phone into my backpack. Then I dig it out and shut it off. My parents say that if I get sent to SAP again they're taking my phone away.

No! No! No!

There's no way I can let that happen.

Phone is off!

But what if something is happening that I need to know about right away? I hate the feeling of not knowing. It makes me feel so . . . out of it.

I turn the phone on.

Then off. Off! Off! Off!

Saturday finally comes. My parents invite Lulu and Vee along with Lulu's mom, Susan; Vee's dad, Tom; and Vee's brother, Eric, to our house to watch the news. Mom makes her famous nachos: One platter is chopped meat, refried beans, cheese, and tortilla chips. Another plateful is chips, veggie refried beans, and cheese, because Lulu and Susan are vegetarians. She also serves a big salad and, my favorite, her mac-and-cheese casserole. We gather around the TV, crowding onto the couch and the extra chairs my parents have put out. "Well, this is exciting!" Susan says with a big smile.

"It sure is," Tom agrees. Susan smiles at him and he smiles back. I text Vee and Lulu.

Megan: Do your parents seem to be acting strange to you?

Lulu: Idk. Are they?

Vee: No. Why?

Megan: Just wondering.

Their parents keep smiling at each other.

"I don't believe this!" my dad says. He sounds fake outraged, like this is something he should be upset about but isn't really. "We're all here together and you girls are still texting, or Snapping, or Instagramming, or whatever it is you're doing. I'd think you'd want to be talking to each other."

"We are talking to each other," Lulu tells him. "We're text talking."

"It's a different world than when we were young," Vee's dad says. He turns to Eric, who is busy on his phone. "And who are you talking to?" he asks Eric.

"Nobody," Eric answers without even looking up. "Video game."

"You're right, Tom. It's a new world," Susan says.

"I wonder if it's better or worse than it was," Tom says.

"It's just different," Susan says.

"Maybe you're right," Tom agrees. They smile at each other again.

Channel 14 News has been playing with the sound off. Mom points the remote at it, bringing the volume up. "It's seven fifteen," she says.

Right on schedule Heather May appears on the screen. She looks taller, and not as thin as she did in person. Plus, her hair is all blown out into a blond halo. She looks very professional in a dark-blue wrap dress. In a way, she doesn't even seem like the same person. "This is Heather May with a special report. Today we'll look at the impact of social media on our kids."

As Heather May starts talking, her voice is over a clip showing people talking, paying bills, playing games, watching videos, and everything else people do on their phones and computers. Heather May tells us about a study that says the brain goes to its happy place every time a person gets a like on something he or she posted. It then shows a bunch of people on their phones, not talking to each other.

Heather May tells us how Snapchat is the most popular social app among teens. "Despite copycat functions on other platforms, Snapping is still the way to go," she says. "How come they're not showing you?" Eric asks. "Are you even in this thing?"

Honestly, I'm getting a little anxious. It's almost over and we haven't appeared. Then, suddenly, there we are. You can really tell we got caught in the rain that day. My hair is all straggly. Megan's is a halo of frizz, and Lulu's hangs in clumps. Again, Heather May's voice comes over the video of us sitting in the SAP room, which really looks like a prison when you see it on TV. "We spoke to a group of girls from Pleasant Hill Middle School. They admitted that their phones play a big part in their lives. They use them to stay in touch with family and friends in the traditional way of calling to talk, but these days there are so many other ways in which phones help them to keep in touch."

The video shows us talking about how we always pay attention to our phones, even during the night. Luckily she doesn't mention that we're in the SAP room because we were using our phones during gym. She shows the part where we tell her that our phones never get in the way of schoolwork. She asks us about all the different social media platforms and ends with Snapchat.

"This is great!" Susan says.

"You girls look great, so cute," my mom adds

"Really?" Vee asks doubtfully. "Look at our hair!"

"It's a mess," I say.

"All three of you are adorable," Susan says.

"I don't know about that," Lulu says, shaking her head. Heather May continues talking to the viewers. "The girls confirmed that Snapping is a lot of fun and that they've even attempted something known as a Snapstreak." The video goes to the part where we're explaining what a Snapstreak is. (My voice is squeaky but not as horrible as I worried it would be.)

As Heather May comes back on, standing in her studio, the adults clap for us. "Nicely done!" Mom says. Our home phone starts ringing right away. I know it's my grandma or my aunts and uncles calling to say they saw me on TV. Everyone's cell phones ring and buzz as people call and text to say they just saw us.

But Heather May is still talking and I catch a few words above the commotion. I tap Vee and Lulu, who are texting. "Listen," I say, pointing to the TV screen.

"In honor of all our Snapstreaking viewers, Channel 14 News is delighted to announce that we've partnered with our affiliate stations to bring you a local contest, and wait until you young people out there hear what the prize will be."

Heather May pauses for dramatic effect. Her smile is brilliant and her eyes sparkle.

"So tell us already," Vee says to the screen.

"The students who can keep a Snapchat Snapstreak going the longest will win a free performance for the students at their schools by the very popular band Boys Being

Dudes," Heather May says. "The contest will end on Saturday two weeks from today."

Vee grabs my arm. Her jaw drops.

Lulu squeezes my shoulder on the opposite side. Her eyes grow ginormous.

I'm glad they're holding on to me because I think I'm going to fall over.

"We. Have. To. Win. This," Vee says in a quiet, intense voice.

"Have. To," Lulu agrees.

"The Snapstreak must be between two students at schools in two different districts. We want this contest to bring kids in the different school districts closer and have them work together. Some experts worry that social media can create social isolation not only among individuals but also among different groups, whose members tend to only interact among themselves. Here at Channel Fourteen we want to see if social media can be used to bring groups together."

Heather May goes on: "The Snapstreak can't have started before the beginning of this week. To enter, go to our website, Channel14News.com, and enter your name and school, along with the name and school of your Snapstreak partner."

Lulu and I both stare at Vee. "Didn't you start Snapping with Gwynneth at the beginning of this week?" I ask.

"Yes," Vee says. "Tuesday."

"And is your streak still going?" Lulu asks.

"Yep," Vee says. "We exchanged Snaps yesterday. She filmed her dog rolling over and I sent her back a video Snap of Heidi Dog running up and down the stairs." Vee checks her phone. The little fire symbol beside Gwynneth's name has a number five in it.

"Yes! Yes! Yes!" I cheer, pumping my arms in the air.

"What's going on?" Dad asks.

"Boys Being Dudes are coming to Pleasant Hill!" I tell him, jumping into the air. Joe the drummer is coming to my school!

Off in the corner I hear Lulu's mother laugh like she's just heard the funniest thing in the world. She's talking to Vee's dad. These two are definitely flirting. (It's so weird when adults do stuff like that. You'd think they would be over all that by their age. It seems so . . . undignified.) I guess they're both single, so they can do what they like. It's still weird to think about, though.

That night I lie awake in bed imagining Joe the drummer and me meeting at Pleasant Hill Middle School while he's there to give the BBD free concert. I'm helping set up. We hit it off right away. He's just crazy about me. He's never met anyone like me. It's magic. He goes on tour, but we write. Years go by and we fall out of touch. Then we meet again later on a city street. In the rain! I'm twenty-four and he's twenty-seven. Our eyes meet and he remembers me from years before. It's magic all over again! We live happily ever after, of course.

The second thing I think about isn't as good. What if Vee's dad and Lulu's mom start dating? Today they sure looked to me like they were heading in that direction. In my waking dream, I imagine Susan in a wedding dress and Tom in a tuxedo. Lulu and Vee are bridesmaids. After the wedding, they drive off together to their new home in Shoreham. Stepsisters!

Leaving me all alone.

Am I being silly? Probably. But they sure did seem to like each other a lot. A lot. A lot. A lot.

CHAPTER 7

THE FIRST THING I do is get in touch with Gwynneth. Luckily I thought fast and used my phone to take a video of Heather May on TV. I Snap it to Gwynneth and write WE CAN WIN THIS!!! at the end.

Sunday is torture! I sit on my bed trying to do math homework but I can't stop checking my phone. It's almost impossible to pay attention to my work.

The four-hour-warning hourglass appears around six at night. Time is almost up. At ten it will be twenty-four hours. If Gwynneth doesn't reply by ten, the streak will be broken and we'll have to start all over again—which pretty much means we won't have a chance to win. I'm sure other kids have started their streaks by now.

Should I send a message to find out why she's not answering me?

Does that make me a pest?

Maybe she's not answering me because she already thinks I'm a pest. What if she's just Snapping back and forth to be nice? What if she only feels sorry for me?

How pathetic!

Oh, these worries! I worry about everything. My mind immediately goes to the worst thing that could happen. I have to stop it! It's not good for me. Maybe Gwynneth simply hasn't looked at her phone. (Ha! As if!) Maybe she lost her phone. (That once happened to me for two days—the two longest days of my life.) Maybe she saw it was from me and thought, Oh no! Not that pesky Vee again! Why won't she bug off!? I'm not answering.

I have to stop!

At 9:42 I glance at my phone and I have one Snap. Gwynneth!!

Who wins the prize? Me? U?

In the fire icon the number five turns to six. Yes! The six-day Snapstreak has been saved! Yes!

Whew! That was close! Now I have twenty-four hours to Snap back. But I still don't know if Gwynneth is willing to do this with me or not.

The Channel 14 News website takes forever before it loads. Come on! Finally it's up. "The Snapstreak contestants duo must attend schools in different districts, but only one free concert will be awarded. It is up to the contestants to decide how and where the concert will be shared," I read out loud from the rules and regulations section.

I take a screenshot and Snap it to Gwynneth.
She responds instantly.

"Let's get hopping—into the winner's circle," she says
with the voice adjuster giving her a low, rumbling voice.

Let's keep talking

Tell me about yourself. I'm all ears!

This is going great! The stuck-up Queen Bee impression I had of Gwynneth at the beginning is changing. She seems kind of fun and wants to actually get to know me.

What will I say about myself?

And then it hits me! This is an unbelievable opportunity. No one knows me at Shoreham. Not yet. I can change anything I don't like about myself just by saying it. It's the chance of a lifetime! I just have to tell Gwynneth and she'll tell everyone else.

Is this dishonest?

Yes.

But I don't have to actually lie. I can just . . . use hyperbole! We learned about it in English class. Hyperbole: exaggeration for the sake of emphasis. I always remember it because I like the way the word sounds. Hyperbole.

Now I have to think carefully. What do I want the kids at Shoreham High to think about me? What would I like to change about myself?

I get off my bed and look at myself in the mirror. I sometimes wish I wasn't quite so tall. Ethan Myers is one of the tallest boys in the eighth grade and he isn't even taller than I am. I know the boys will all have a growth spurt later on, but I'm even tall among the girls. It can feel awkward towering over everyone else. There's not much I can change about that, though.

But if I can't change my height . . . I can pretend I have an awesome career as a model. Why not? I love fashion.

People say I'm pretty, that I should model. So what if I have no photos? I'm a runway model. Definitely!

That's a good one.

Am I popular? Not super popular. I'm normal popular. I have my close friends, Lulu and Megan. I say hi and chat with a bunch of other people, too. I don't get invited to every single party but to enough of them. I could present myself as being MORE popular.

One of my faults is impatience. I am extremely impatient. I know that about myself, and once again, I'm now impatient to get started on my new image makeover. (That's it! It's not dishonesty, it's an image makeover.)

Sitting back down on my bed, I begin Snapping back to Gwynneth.

5 things about me
(since you're all ears, lol!)

Then I type this:

V-Ness

1. I was a child model and I still model. Mostly runway modeling.
2. I was almost elected class president. I lost by one vote.
3. I love lacrosse. I play on the JV team even though I'm still in 8th grade.
4. I once appeared on a dancing competition show.
5. I can't wait to start school at Shoreham High.

I read it over and decide it's not lies. I could be a model if I got discovered or someone showed me how to apply. I ran for class president and didn't lose by a ton of votes. I do love lacrosse and plan to try out for the high school team. I've taken dance lessons since I was six and I'm a good dancer, so it could happen someday that I manage to appear on TV.

How likely am I to get caught in these lies? I added the part about being a runway model so I don't have to produce print ads. I didn't claim to be class president, and I did run. They don't list the names of girls' lacrosse team players on the school website. And I only said I appeared on the dance show. I didn't say I competed. I think I'm safe.

The only real, true lie is number five. I'm scared to death to go to Shoreham High in the fall.

My door is open and Dad knocks. "Come on in," I say, putting down my phone on the bed next to me. He sits on the edge. Heidi Dog scampers in and settles by his feet.

The concerned expression on Dad's face makes me worry. "What's up?" I ask.

"I just got off the phone with the real estate agent, and there's been a new development," he says.

"We're not moving?" I ask eagerly. "That's okay. I can live with that! Not a problem."

He smiles, but sadly. "No. The opposite. A couple has made an offer on this place if they can move in by the end of this month."

"End of the month?!" I cry out. "That's only three weeks away!"

"I know. But I need someone who can move in right away. I can't afford to make two mortgage payments."

"Move in three weeks! That's crazy! There's three months of school left. No way, Dad! I'm not going!"

"I'm sorry, Vee. I didn't expect this either," Dad says.

His phone rings and he fishes it from his back pocket. It says SUSAN VANCE. "Why is Lulu's mother calling you?" I ask.

Dad gets a shifty look, like he's embarrassed about something. "I left her a message and she's calling me back."

"Answer the phone," I say.

"She'll leave a message. I'll call her later. You and I are talking now." The call goes to voicemail. I hope Lulu is all right. I can't imagine what else he and she could be talking about. Thinking about Lulu reminds me of something. "I'll live with Lulu! She invited me to," I tell him.

"What?" Dad couldn't look more shocked. "What?"

I never mentioned it to him before because I knew he'd say no. And I wasn't so sure I wanted to do that, anyway. The pigsty of a room and all. But now everything has changed.

I can't leave school before the end of the year. I simply cannot. It's one thing to be the new kid on the first day of ninth grade, when everyone is new to the high school— that's tough enough. But to come in toward the end of eighth grade? It's just . . . unthinkable.

"Does Susan know about this?" Dad asks.

"Lulu asked her. She's thinking about it," I say. "I'm sure it will be all right." More hyperbole. But I'm desperate.

"Susan never mentioned this to me," Dad says.

"Maybe she . . . uh . . . forgot," I say. "Since when are you guys such buddies that she tells you everything?"

"We're not, but we spoke at the Hardwicks' house yesterday and then again this afternoon. I'd imagine it would have come up. That's strange," Dad says.

"What did you talk about today?" I ask.

"Oh, this and that. We had a pleasant conversation yesterday and I simply wanted to get to continue it." I scratch my head. This is odd. I can't think about it, though. I have more important things to concern myself with.

Dad gets up off the bed. "I know it's a lot to deal with, Vee. I'm sorry. Now I have to go tell Eric. I'm sure he won't be any happier about it than you are."

Is he kidding?! Eric! Eric will barely even notice that he's in a different school as long as he has his video games. I'm the one who's in a crisis here.

Dad kisses me on the top of my head and leaves. I realize that I've been using Gwynneth as a distraction, trying to convince myself that if I befriend her, everything will be all right. But it won't be all right. Gwynneth or no Gwynneth—I'm going to miss my friends at Pleasant Hill, especially Megan and Lulu. I've been with most of them since kindergarten. Kindergarten! And I was planning on graduating from high school with them, as well.

I was only kidding myself, thinking I could create a different me, a more popular, athletic, glamorous me. My classmates know me and most of them like me as I am. That's worth a lot more than asking new kids to like some made-up phony self. What was I thinking?

From the floor, Heidi Dog whimpers to be picked up. She's too short to climb onto my bed on her own. Leaning over, I lift her and plunk her down beside me. "That's a good girl," I say, scratching her between the ears. It would be kind of tough leaving Heidi Dog behind if I go live with Lulu, but it wouldn't be forever.

Heidi Dog can't seem to find a comfortable spot. She walks all over the bed. Her brush is on my dresser so I go get it. Maybe brushing her will settle her down. It might settle both of us down.

Even though it's past ten o'clock, I'm dying to talk to Lulu. I know she's still up. She always is, even though she's not supposed to be on her phone after ten. (Neither am I, actually.) I have to at least text her, though. I need to know if I can live with her.

Heidi Dog has finally found a comfy spot and I begin brushing her. She stretches out. She loves being brushed.

I'm so confused about the whole living-with-Lulu thing. Part of me wants to do it. It would be better than moving. And another part of me doesn't want to be separated from my family. Maybe if I discuss it with Lulu things will seem clearer.

Before I do that, I have to delete that stupid Snap I was about to send Gwynneth. What a dumb idea! I must have been crazy. It would have been impossible to keep all those lies going. And how embarrassing if I got caught!

My phone doesn't seem to be on the bed where I'm sure I put it down. Leaning off the side, I search underneath. No. Not there. "That's strange, Heidi Dog," I say. "Where could my phone have gone?"

That's when I see a light glowing beneath Heidi Dog. There it is! My dog has been sitting on my phone all this time. Gently I move Heidi Dog and pick up my phone.

And I see a PINK ARROW.

OMG! It sent! The five big whopping lies I was about to tell Gwynneth. That I DID JUST TELL GWYN-NETH!!!!!!!!!!!!!!!!!!!!!!!!!!!!!!!!!!!!!!

I feel totally sick inside. Now what?!

CHAPTER 8

So Vee sends me this strange Snap just as I'm about to turn off my lamp and go to sleep. I can't ignore it because she needs me.

Luloony

What? What? What's the matter?

V-Ness

Did your mom decide if I can live with you or not?
I need to know now!!!!

Luloony

What's the rush?

V-Ness

Dad says we have to move by the end of the month

Luloony

!!!

V-Ness

I know!!!!! Did you ask?

The truth is . . . I didn't ask. I didn't think Mom would agree to it, and I don't think Vee's dad would say yes, either. Do I want to live with Vee? Yes and no. If Vee lives with Mom and me she won't have to move. That's the yes part. Do I want to share my room with Vee? Not really. Vee is a bit of a neat freak. Her bedroom always looks like the clean squad just swept through. I don't know how she lives like that. To me, my bedroom is the only place in the house that's mine alone. Mom encourages me to be tidier, but she doesn't actually enforce it. Vee would insist I clean up. (She can be very bossy sometimes.) And then it wouldn't feel like my room anymore. I'm a creative person. When I'm in the middle of a drawing, I can't be expected keep my colored pencils in an orderly line. If I write a poem longhand on a pad, I need to be able to tear out the pages that aren't right and throw them away. If the trash can is filled, I can't stop to empty it. I would break my creative flow. When I finish my artistic projects, the last thing I want to do is clean up. I'm too worn out.

But what kind of friend would I be if I didn't at least ask Mom if Vee can stay? Not a very good one.

Luloony

I'll go ask Mom if she's decided yet.

V-Ness

Thnx. You are the best. Got to 😜

Luloony

Kk. See you tomorrow.

Stepping into the hall, I check to see if the light is still on under Mom's bedroom door. It is! From outside her door, I hear that she's talking to someone on the phone. Laughing. There's also a second voice. She's on speakerphone.

Should I knock? I wait a few minutes. More laughing. I can't stand out here all night.

"Come in," she answers when I knock.

She sits on top of her bed in her pajamas, her phone on the bed beside her. "One second," she says to the person on the other end.

"I have a question," I say. She raises her eyebrows as if to ask what my question is. "It's not a quick question," I add.

A male voice comes from her phone. "Go ahead. I'll call you tomorrow."

I look sharply at the phone. I know that voice. But from where?

"Okay. Good night," Mom says to the phone.

"Who is that?" I ask. I don't mean to sound judgmental or disapproving, but that's how my voice comes out. I have no reason to disapprove. Mom and Dad have been divorced for more than two years. Mom can have man friends—even a boyfriend—if she wants to. I'm just . . . I don't know . . . surprised.

"Just a friend," Mom answers me. "What's your question?"

So I sit beside her on the bed and explain about how Vee has to move in a month and can she live with us. "Live with us?" Mom says. "We don't have an extra bedroom."

"We could get another bed into my room," I suggest.

Mom laughs hard. "I can't even get into your bedroom," she says.

"I would clean up," I say. For some reason I feel offended, though I'm not sure why. I suppose a person doesn't like another person to say she's messy even when she knows she is.

"I don't know, Lulu. Is her dad okay with this plan?"

"Mmm . . . he isn't actually aware of it yet," I admit.

"I had a feeling that was the case. Let me think about it."

"All right, but you have to think fast," I say. "She needs to know."

"Are you sure this is what you want?" Mom asks me.

"Of course it is, Mom! Vee is my best friend, plus Megan. I don't want her to move. What will I do if she moves?"

"You still have Megan. Besides, you and Vee can stay in touch. Plus you can make other friends."

"No! No! No, Mom! You don't understand how it works. Megan and I won't stay friends if Vee isn't here."

"Why not?"

"That's just how it is."

"You can make new friends."

"No, I can't. I'm not good at that!" I say.

Mom's face creases into a look of surprise. "Why do you think that?"

"Because I haven't made a new friend since the sixth grade. It's Megan, Vee, and me."

"The Three Amigas, the Three Musketeers, the Three Stooges," Mom says.

I have no idea what she's talking about but I get the idea. Groups of things in threes. "Yes!" I say.

"Maybe you should expand your circle of friends to more than two," Mom says.

I don't want to hear it. Plus it's late and I need some sleep. Lacrosse again tomorrow, and my phone says to expect sunny skies. There's no escape this time.

"It would be fun to have Vee here," I tell Mom. "Please say yes."

"I'm thinking," Mom says. "Good night." She blows me a kiss.

I blow one back. "Night."

I climb into bed, really tired now. I settle under the covers and realize that I'm smiling. Why? Nothing so great has happened—at least not yet. And there's lacrosse tomorrow. So why am I so happy?

I imagine how Gwynneth will feel when she learns that Vee isn't moving to Shoreham after all.

I've won! I've destroyed Gwynneth, my archenemy! She won't be able to steal my best friend! She's been vanquished, smooshed, eliminated!

THAT'S why I'm smiling!

CHAPTER 9

JOE THE DRUMMER is on my mind. Is it crazy to obsess over a celebrity crush? Yes! Totally. Can I stop? No! Believe me, I'm trying. Trying! Trying! Trying! Boy, am I ever trying!

It's no use!

If I have any shot at all of making this dream come true, I have to give Vee all the support I can. We're going to win this because we have nearly a week's lead on everyone else. The only way we can lose is if either Gwynneth or Vee messes up the Snapstreak for some reason. I can't think of any reason why either of them would do that, so . . . Joe the drummer, here I come.

I put my sneakers next to my pack so I don't have to

go searching for them in the morning and I'm off to bed, eager to continue dreaming about Joe the drummer.

On the bus the next morning, Vee and Lulu barely notice me when I get on and slide into my usual seat in front of them. Turning to face them, I hear them chatting excitedly about the possibility that Vee will move in with Lulu. "I'll come over this afternoon to help you clean up your room," Vee says to Lulu. "That way your mom will see that I'm a good influence on you and she'll be more inclined to say I can stay."

"I can help," I say, suddenly feeling left out.

"I don't need you guys to help," Lulu says. "I can clean my own room."

"But you won't," Vee says. "That's the whole point. With me around you will. Your mom will see that."

"And me too," I add, not really sure what I mean by that. "She'll be glad I'm helping, too."

"I like my room the way it is," Lulu says.

Vee's eyes go wide. I laugh just a little because I can see what's going on here. "I'd invite you to live with me, Vee," I say, "but my parents wouldn't go for it. Dad would never agree to have another person eating our groceries, which he says are 'overpriced.'"

Vee laughs. "That's okay. I understand."

"Does Gwynneth know you're not moving to Shoreham?" I ask.

Vee shakes her head. "When it's definite, I'll have to tell—"

"No!" I cut her off. "Gwynneth must never know you're not coming to Shoreham."

"She's going to find out eventually," Vee says.

"Okay, but eventually, not now," I say. "If Gwynneth knows you're not coming to Shoreham, she won't want to be your friend anymore and she won't bother keeping up the Snapstreak."

"Why wouldn't she want to be my friend?" Vee asks, looking hurt.

"Maybe she would," I say. I feel bad that I've hurt her feelings, but I have to be honest. "She might not, though. If you're not going to be around, why bother?"

"I don't know," Vee says doubtfully. "She'll still want to win the prize, won't she?"

"I suppose," I say. "Let's not take any chances, though. I say you shouldn't tell her, just in case."

"In case of what?" Lulu asks.

"There's still a chance your mom will decide I can't live with you," Vee says to Lulu. "I'll wait until it's definite to tell Gwynneth."

Vee is wearing her new sparkly gold sneakers. "Aren't you worried you'll mess those up out on the field during lacrosse?" I ask.

"A little," Vee replies, "but I want one of you to take a video of me playing lacrosse today. I'll Snap it to Gwynneth."

"I'll do it," Lulu says. "You know I'm always on the sidelines during gym."

"Does that hurt your feelings?" I ask Lulu. She's one of the worst players, and Vee is almost always a team captain. Vee picks her but hardly ever plays her, except at the very end because Ms. Pate wants everyone to play, at least a little.

"I don't play you because I don't think you really want to run around," Vee says.

"It's true! I don't!" Lulu says. "The sideline is fine. I prefer it there."

"See?" Vee says to me. "Don't get caught," she tells Lulu, "just try to catch ten good seconds."

"Aye, aye, captain!" Lulu jokes.

Vee's phone buzzes. She takes it from the front pocket of her backpack. As soon as she sees who's texted her she flushes pink.

"It's Ethan Myers, isn't it?" Lulu guesses. "I could tell from the way you're blushing."

"I'm not blushing," Vee says, even though clearly, she is. She always blushes when the subject of Ethan Myers comes up. "He says he wants to go with me to the BBD concert if someone from our school wins it," she tells us.

"Nooooooooooooooooooo way!!!!!!!!" Lulu says, thumping Vee's shoulder excitedly. "A date, Vee! That would be a date!"

"No it wouldn't," Vee says as she sends a return text.

I strain my neck to see what she's typing but I can't get a good look. "What are you telling him?"

"I'm saying let's see if I win first," Vee tells me.

"Oh, that's cool," Lulu says with admiration.

"Would you go with him if you win?" I ask.

"Would she go with him?!" Lulu cries out. "What kind of question is that?! Of course she would. Vee has liked Ethan since sixth grade. He's finally paying attention to her. He one-hundred-percent absolutely likes you, Vee."

Vee gets another text. "He says he'll see me at gym," she tells us. She smiles, pleased. She knows she's a good player and will look good out there.

A Snap comes in. "Gwynneth," Vee reports. She looks at it quickly and then sticks it into the pocket of her backpack.

"Let's see," I say.

"It's nothing," Vee says.

"Then show us," Lulu says.

"I told you it wasn't important," Vee insists.

"Okay, be that way," Lulu says, scowling.

It's not like Vee to keep texts and Snaps and things like that secret. What could have been in that Snap?

CHAPTER 10

VEE

I'VE BEEN KIND of a wreck ever since Heidi Dog sent my five big lies to Gwynneth.

The Snap worked. Gwynneth was SUPER impressed. She started chatting me immediately:

GQB2the2ndpwr

> I'm going to tell EVERYONE at Shoreham Middle all about your awesomeness. Come visit over the summer. All my friends are dying to meet u! Bring modeling shots.

I absolutely can't go to Shoreham now. I'll either have to admit I lied—a lot—or I have to keep these lies going for the rest of my life! Both those possibilities make my stomach twist.

I'm glad we have gym first period today. Playing lacrosse will keep me too busy to think about anything else but moving the ball up the field. For forty-five minutes all I have to think about is scoring.

Even though Pleasant Hill Middle School isn't the fanciest place, it has great athletic fields. There is a track that goes around the football field. Today, while we girls play lacrosse, the boys are out running on the track.

On the sideline, Lulu keeps trying to take a video of me. She's attempting to be sneaky about it so Ms. Pate won't see that she has a phone. She holds the phone low, tilting it upward. Girls keep getting in her way, blocking her view of me.

I feel guilty that I asked her to do this. If she gets caught with the phone again she'll go to SAP. Her mom won't be happy, and if she finds out it was because of me . . . That won't help convince her that I would be the greatest roommate for Lulu. I want to take it back, tell her to put the phone away, but I can't get to her now.

Lulu keeps checking on Ms. Pate, which makes her look really guilty. If Ms. Pate notices Lulu she'll be able to tell in an instant that Lulu is up to something, just from the sneaky way she's skulking around. I can't even concentrate on the game; I'm so busy watching Ms. Pate and

Lulu, as well as keeping an eye out for Ethan. This wasn't a good idea at all!

The boys have come out and are jogging around the track. I catch sight of Ethan, but he doesn't notice me. I stop for a moment to watch him jog. He really is the cutest.

I picked Megan to be on my team and I see her coming up the midfield line. She notices that I'm open and shoots the lacrosse ball to me. Catching it in my net, I race up the field. (I hope Ethan is seeing all of this.) Just as I'm about to score, two girls on the opposing team rush toward me. Megan is open, so I toss the ball back to her.

Ethan is coming around the bend. I smooth my hair.

He waves.

I wave back and smile.

Has Megan made the goal? I turn back to find out.

WHAM! The lacrosse ball smashes right into my forehead.

OOOOOOOOOOOOOOOOwwwwwwww! I drop to my knees. The ground around me spins. Then a black hole opens and swallows me whole.

When I open my eyes I'm lying on my back on the grass staring up into Ms. Pate's worried eyes. My classmates surround her, all gaping down at me. "She's awake!" Megan cries out. She's kneeling by my shoulder. Lulu is jumping up and down at the back of the crowd, trying to see over their heads.

They all squeeze closer, but Ms. Pate tells them to get back. "Give her air," she says.

A siren screams, getting louder and louder. A spinning red light appears above the heads of the girls. "I don't need an ambulance," I say, although my head really hurts. I struggle up onto my elbows to prove I'm okay.

"Lie down and don't talk," Ms. Pate says, putting her hand on the back of my neck and guiding me down to the ground.

Megan sighs deeply. "I'm so sorry, Vee, so, so, so sorry. I thought you saw me toss the ball to you."

"It's okay," I say and a shot of pain crosses my forehead.

A man and woman, the emergency medical team, hurry out onto the field carrying a stretcher. "I really don't need to go to the hospital," I say to the EMTs.

"You're going, Vee, so don't argue," Ms. Pate says.

Carefully, they lift me and place me on the stretcher. I can't believe this is happening. It's so dramatic. Like on TV!

The EMTs carry me through the open back doors of the ambulance. Ms. Pate climbs in beside me. The woman medic sits beside her as the man medic slams the back doors shut. The motor starts. We zoom away from the school with the sirens blaring.

It's so unreal!

The medic whose name tag says LAUREN shines a penlight into my eyes. "Her pupils are dilated," Lauren tells Ms. Pate. "She might have a concussion. How long was she unconscious?"

Unconscious! Now I really feel like a TV character. I never knew anyone who was unconscious. Will I get amnesia? That always happens on TV when characters are clonked on the head. I know my own name. I recognize Ms. Pate. I don't have amnesia yet, but it might set in later.

I'd find this all pretty amazing and interesting if my head didn't hurt so much. The pain is not only in the front but also at the base of my head, in the back where my neck and head meet.

When we get to the hospital, the medics rush me into the emergency room. It's all kind of a blur. They take pictures of my brain in something called a CAT scan. (Strange name. I imagine kittens pawing my hair as they examine my head.) They have me draw pictures of clocks. I keep trying to draw a round clock but my clock keeps coming out more like a fat worm. Putting the numbers into the clock is surprisingly difficult, too. The number six at the bottom slips out of the clock altogether. I wonder why I can't do it.

Maybe I'm forgetting what a clock looks like. Amnesia alert!

Then, while I'm resting in the exam room with Ms. Pate keeping me company, a hot rumbling swirls in my belly. In the next second I'm upchucking in the trash can. It's pretty embarrassing. But Ms. Pate is nice. A nurse brings me a glass of water and then carries out the can.

The doctor and nurse return to the examination room. I tell them I puked. (As if they couldn't tell from the stink.) The doctor and nurse look at each other, as if puking is meaningful. "Is that normal?" I ask. "After you get hit in the head, I mean."

"It can be," the doctor answers.

All I really want to do is sleep, so as soon as the doctor and nurse leave the room I turn my back on Ms. Pate and stretch out on the examination table. As I drift off, it hits me that my backpack isn't in the room. Who has it? Did they leave it on the field? My phone is in it!

It's so weird not to have my phone. Megan and Lulu will want to know how I am. Maybe Ethan will even call or text me.

"Has anyone called my dad?" I ask Ms. Pate.

"I did," she says. "He just left me a message. He's stuck in traffic."

The nurse comes in and picks up a chart lying on the desk. "Where's my phone?" I ask. "Can I have it?"

"I'll go see if it's at the nurses' station," he says, leaving.

A moment later he returns and hands it to me.

"Thanks," I say. "I hate being without it."

"I know how you feel," the nurse says. "We're not allowed to use them while we're working."

Dad rushes in. His right eye is twitching like it always does when he's upset. "Are you okay, Vee?" he asks.

"I've been better," I say.

Ms. Pate updates him on everything that's happened. He listens, nodding. As she speaks he looks more and more distressed. I don't want to upset him even more but I'm feeling pretty terrible even though the throbbing headache is slightly improved from the medicine the nurse gave me.

"Can we go home?" I ask.

Dad looks really worried. "I'll go get the doctor," the nurse says.

"I'll come with you," Ms. Pate tells him. They leave and I sit there trying to keep my eyes open. (I'm relieved that I recognize Dad. No amnesia yet.) Sleepy though I am, I also want to check my phone. I have two Snaps.

One is from Gwynneth, of course. It's a video she took while walking down the hall in her school. It's just kids walking, just shoes. Actually, it's kind of funny. She's added little mice icons running around as if they're underfoot in the hallway.

The next Snap is from Lulu. She took a video of me being hit on the head. Ow! Seeing it makes my head hurt all over again. At the part where I fall down, she's added stars and cuckoo-bird sounds.

Lulu: Okay?

Vee: Idk. Head hurts.

The pain gets even worse as I stare at my phone.

"Maybe you should put that phone down for now," Dad says. "Just relax."

A million reasons why I have to be on the phone pop into my head but I don't have the energy to argue. "Okay," I say, setting my phone aside. Ms. Pate returns with the doctor. She says she'll be going back to school now that Dad is there. She says she'll call Dad later to see how I'm doing. Dad shakes her hand as she leaves and thanks her for all she's done for me. I thank her, too.

"We want to watch you overnight," the doctor reports after Ms. Pate has gone. "We'd like you to spend the night in the hospital for observation. We're going to run a few more tests."

"Am I all right?" I ask. "The words on my cell phone got all shaky."

"We're pretty sure you have a concussion," the doctor tells us. I've heard about concussions before but I'm not a hundred percent sure what it means.

"Is that like amnesia?" I ask.

Dad squints his eyes and looks at me strangely.

"You know," I say, "like people get on TV."

"No, it's not amnesia. Your brain got rattled around in your skull when the ball hit you," the doctor says. "Then when you fell backwards, your head got hit a second time."

That explains why it hurts in both places. "I'll be okay, though, right?" I ask.

"Yes, but you have to rest."

That's fine with me. All I want to do is sleep right now.

"You're going to have to take some time off from school," the doctor says. No problem there. It gives me more time to think of Snaps to send Gwynneth.

"We're going to want you to rest your brain and your eyes," the doctor adds.

"How do I do that?" I ask.

The doctor nods toward the phone I hold in my hands. "The first thing is no electronics for a while."

"Wha . . . What?" I sputter.

"That's right," says the doctor. "No laptop, no tablet, and no phone. It's too great a strain on your mind and your eyes. The key word here is *rest*. You need lots of sleep and relaxation."

"I can't do that," I say. "I'm in a Snapstreak competition. My entire school is depending on me to keep the streak going. We have to win this free concert by BBD."

"What's BBD?" the doctor asks.

Is she kidding?! How could she not know BBD?! "Boys Being Dudes," I tell her.

"Sorry that you'll miss the dudes," the doctor says. "The electronic screen is very hard on your eyes. Doing all that typing takes more focus than you might realize. I suggest that you even restrict your TV watching."

What am I supposed to do? Stare at the walls all day? More important than that is my Snapstreak. Everyone is counting on me. Gwynneth is counting on me. "But the concert," I say, my voice getting high and whiny.

"Your health is more important than some concert," the doctor says.

Some concert!!!!! She so totally doesn't get it! "This might not seem important, but believe me, this is really, really important. I'll be letting down my whole school! And not only that—"

"Vee," Dad cuts me off. "You heard the doctor."

I heard her loud and clear, even though I wish I hadn't.

There has to be a way around this. I won't Snap until I see the hourglass pop up. "I'll be better in about a day, won't I?" I ask the doctor.

The doctor smiles but shakes her head. "We're talking about weeks, maybe months. It will all depend on what symptoms do or don't develop in the next few weeks. We'll be watching you closely. It's crucial that you don't get hit on the head again. So absolutely no gym or sports or anything physical. This is serious. You must rest."

Getting whacked in the head with a lacrosse ball might make my head hurt for a while, but being without my phone is going to KILLLLLLLLLLLLLLLLLLL me for sure!

CHAPTER 11

SHOES! I CAN'T believe I sent Vee a video of shoes!
Not even cool shoes, either, like her golden sparkle sneakers. No! Just crummy old shoes, mostly sneakers. Like . . .
what was I thinking?!

What I was thinking was this: I'd better send Vee
something before time runs out. I was, like, blank, you
know? Every time I have to send Vee a Snap I totally stress.
She is the coolest person ever and she totally thinks I'm
also cool. Which is such a laugh.

It's hysterical, really.

If she only knew where I was coming from when I met
her that day in front of Emma's old house. Lucy, Kayla,
Ava, and I were coming back from a Mathletes tourna-

ment! (Which we rocked, BTW.) Here's a screenshot of the Snap I sent to everyone that day.

I didn't send it to Vee, though. There was something about her. I could just tell she was a cool girl. Like, she hadn't even moved into Emma's house yet and she acted like she already owned the block. If I had to go to a new neighborhood and some strange girls came up to talk to me . . . I would melt. I wouldn't know what to say. I might even run away. Not Vee, though. She just like stood there . . . cool, as cool could be.

And then I learn all this amazing stuff about her. She's a model! She plays JV lacrosse in the eighth grade. She's like Super Girl or something.

I so desperately want us to be friends!

A cool friend is just the thing I've been hoping for. It's as though Vee fell from the sky, an answer to my prayers. I've been looking to, like, change my image but didn't know how to begin. I had all that eyeliner on the day I met Vee because I was experimenting. I wanted to see what kind of impression I'd make with some makeup on among new kids and I totally overdid it with the eyes. Lucy, Kayla, and Ava told me it looked good, but maybe they were just being nice.

The whole GQB2the2ndpwr Snapchat name was a total goof. Emma and I made it up because we thought it was funny—the idea of a Queen Bee Mathlete. Vee didn't get it; she thinks I really am some kind of Queen Bee. I didn't mean for her to come to the wrong conclusion. But since she did . . .

Now I have to keep this image going. How am I ever going to do that? It's not easy to keep pretending I'm something that I'm not—GQB2the2ndpwr, cool girl.

I'm telling you it's, like, exhausting. I always have to remember to put that eyeliner on every time I take a picture to put on Snapchat. (My mother totally forbids me to wear eyeliner until I'm in high school, and even then, she's not in love with the idea, so I have to put the eyeliner on and then take it off right away before she sees me wearing it. Yesterday I took it off without a mirror and had it smeared over my face without my knowing. When my mother questioned me I told her I was trying out for the part of a raccoon in the school play.)

So, according to my calculations, if I can get Vee to be my friend AND win this concert of these guys, Boys Being Dudes . . . or whoever they are (I don't pay that much attention to the radio, even though I play the violin), it all adds up to me having a cooler image when I start high school in the fall.

But I have to keep thinking of these Snaps to send. Help! I'm out of ideas.

Checking my phone I see that the little hourglass has popped up again. Why is Vee taking so long to answer? It's the shoes! She hates the shoes. She thinks I'm a total nerd. Why did I ever send her those shoes?

A purple box just popped up on Snapchat! Yay! It has to be Vee. I have to answer fast.

Oh no! It's a video of her being hit in the head with a lacrosse ball! Wow! She's knocked right off her feet. Ouch! She follows it up with a chat:

V-Ness

If my dad finds out I'm sending you this I will be in so much trouble.

See? She's a tough girl AND a rebel. Nothing gets her down. Like . . . how can I ever hope to measure up to that?

CHAPTER 12

MEGAN

SITTING ON THE edge of my bed, I text Vee.

Megawatt: V? You 😴 ?

No answer. Lulu texts me.

Luloony: V is still at the hospital.

Megawatt: How do you know?

Luloony: Mom talked to her dad.

Megawatt: What's w them?

Luloony: They were talking about V's head injury

Megawatt: V ok?

Luloony: Concession

Megawatt: Wha? Like a hot dog stand?
Did she get a bad hot dog?

Luloony: Ugh! Autocorrect! Concussion

Megawatt: OMG!! Sounds bad.

Luloony: Way bad. She needs to rest. Dad took away her phone

Megawatt: 👻 NO!!!!!!!!!!!!!!!!!!!!!!!!!!!!! What about BBD???!!!! How long will she have to rest?

Luloony: I don't know but this is bad.

Megawatt: BAD!!!!!

My phone suddenly buzzes. It's Vee. How did she get her phone? "Vee!" I cry out as I click onto the call. "How do you feel?"

On the other end, a little hiccup of a whimper rolls up into a giant sob and then fades out again into a pathetic sigh. "Horrible."

"I thought your dad took your phone."

"He did," she says. "But he's asleep so I took it back. I had to send Gwynneth a Snap before time ran out. I sent Lulu's video of me getting cracked in the head." Vee sniffs and starts crying again.

"Don't cry, Vee," I say. "We'll figure something out." My eyes fill with tears. It always happens to me when someone else starts to cry.

"I don't care what the doctor or Dad wants," Vee says in a choked voice. "When he goes to work, I'll get my phone."

"But you're supposed to be resting."

"I don't need to rest!" Vee is really crying hard now. She might think she doesn't need to rest but she sounds super wiped out to me. "I have to go. I'm going to puke again," Vee says and the call goes dead.

Wow.

My fingers fly across the keyboard of my laptop as I Google. I want to know what could happen to Vee if she doesn't take her concussion recovery seriously.

Here's what I learn: An untreated concussion could make her unable to do her schoolwork because her vision could blur and her eyes would get tired when she tried to read; she could have headaches and neck pain that doesn't go away; she might always feel tired and she might start to act emotionally unstable and irritable; she could develop depression, anxiety, and irrational fears; Vee could become mentally ill; she could develop epilepsy, which I know causes people to have uncontrollable seizures. She might suffer from dizziness for the rest of her life.

The rest of her life!

This is way, way, way more serious than I would have guessed. I can't let Vee ignore the doctor's orders. This is really upsetting. I text Lulu.

Megan: Just searched concussion. Scary! Vee HAS TO REST! 🖐

Lulu: Searching . . . OMG!!!! This is nuts! Scary feels.

Megan: Way serious. No fooling with this! I feel guilty, guilty, guilty!

Lulu: It's not your fault.

After saying goodbye to Lulu, I continue to sit on my bed, thinking. Lulu and I have to make sure Vee rests. What kinds of friends would we be if we didn't? Selfish friends, that's what kind. It's such a shame, though. To think that we almost had Boys Being Dudes playing right on our performing arts center stage! (I imagine Joe the drummer onstage in the PAC, beaming a smile from behind his drum set to me as I bop along in the first row.)

There has to be a way to keep the Snapstreak going. Of course there's a way! A great idea strikes me. Grabbing my phone, I send Lulu a Snap.

I'm a genius!

CHAPTER 13

I DON'T EVEN LIKE Gwynneth! Of course, I don't know her, but I don't like the idea of her.

And I don't like the look of her, either. All that eyeliner! Queen Bee types really bug me.

They're only nice to their own hive, and even then, not so much. I don't know how they even rise to that position. They're kind of bullies, if you ask me.

This is why I don't love Megan's idea when she runs it past me. This is her big stroke of genius—that she and I take charge of Vee's phone and keep up the Snapstreak pretending to be Vee.

First of all, how are we getting the phone away from Vee's dad?

Second, what do I have to say to GQB2the2ndpwr? NOTHING!

This is a lot to think about and it's making me hungry, even though it's almost midnight. I head downstairs to see what's in the fridge. Mom is already there, sitting at the kitchen table, staring down at a bowl of cereal. "Why are you up?" she asks when I come in.

"Why are YOU up?" I say as I take a bowl from the cabinet.

"Stuff to think about," Mom says.

"Are you thinking about if Vee can live with us?" I ask, sitting beside her.

Mom sighs. That's not good. "I don't think it's a great idea," she says.

"Moooooooooooooooooooooooooooom!!!!" I say.

"Luluuuuuuuuuuuuuuuuuuuuuuuuuuuuuu!!!!" she replies.

"Don't mock me," I say. "Why can't she stay with us?"

"We don't have enough room, Lulu. We don't have an extra room for Vee and your bedroom is such a mess that I don't know how you even find your bed at night."

"I'll be neater," I say. She rolls her eyes in disbelief. "Really," I add. "I can do it."

Mom keeps her doubtful expression.

I stand, offended. "I can't believe your lack of faith in me," I say in a hurt voice. "I'm going to bed."

"If you can find it," Mom mumbles under her breath. I whirl back to face her. "What did you say?" I ask, even though I heard her.

Mom grins guiltily. "Sorry. Kidding. Sweet dreams."

"Really, I can be neater," I say.

"Good. I hope so," she says. I know she doesn't believe it one bit. And I'm not sure I do, either.

The next day Vee isn't in school, which I expected. During lunch, Megan and I send her a Snap of the gross meatloaf they served that day. We do this even though her dad took her phone. I have faith in her ability to find it again, just like she did the other day.

A bunch of kids see what we're doing and want to be in the video. They clutch their necks and pretend to choke. Ethan Myers acts like he's poisoned. "Sorry you're hurt but be glad you're missing this meatloaf," he says.

"How romantic," Megan whispers to me.

"Isn't it?" I say.

"Maybe she won't even see this," Megan says.

"Oh, she'll find her phone," I say. "I have faith in our girl."

"She should really be resting," Megan says.

"When she's rested, she'll find her phone and then

she'll see it," I reply. I can't believe Vee has to be cut off from civilization just because she got hit on the head. It seems cruel and inhumane.

"I don't know," Megan says in a worried voice.

I send the Snap. It would be worse for Vee to believe we weren't thinking of her. She wouldn't want to miss a video with Ethan in it, even if he was being goofy.

During classes I keep my phone on mute and ask to go to the girls' room to check. Nothing. Between classes I lean into my locker for coverage and sneak a peek. No reply. I wonder if this time her father hid her phone somewhere where she can't find it.

"It's possible she's sleeping," Megan says as she comes alongside me.

"That must be it," I say. There's no way Vee wouldn't respond to a Snap video masterpiece like this. At dismissal there's still no word from her. Megan and I decide we'd better get over there ASAP to see if she's okay.

When we get to Vee's house, we notice that her dad's car isn't in the driveway. "Maybe he went to work," Megan says.

"That would be good. It gives her a chance to find her phone," I say.

Eric opens the door. "Is Vee awake?" I ask as we step inside.

"She's definitely not sleeping," he tells us.

"How do you know?" Megan asks.

"Listen," Eric says, pointing toward the stairs. "Aaahhh!!" Vee shouts.

Megan and I race up the stairs, leaving Eric behind. "Vee, what's wrong?" I shout down the hallway.

We find her in her dad's room sitting on the corner of the bed, slumped over. "He has to have hidden it here somewhere," she says.

"Your phone?" Megan asks, sitting beside her.

Vee nods. "I think he knows I took it from his room last night."

"Of course he knows," I say, joining them on the bed. "He just has to look at the time stamps on your texts."

"I thought he respected my privacy too much to do that," Vee says.

"He probably figured you wouldn't snoop around in his room for your phone, either," I reply.

"Maybe he took it to work with him," Megan says.

"He didn't go to work," Vee says. "He just ran out to the store. He'll be back soon. This is my only chance to find my phone while he's out."

"Maybe he put your stuff in the car. My mom always hides birthday presents and stuff in the trunk of her car," Megan says.

Vee's eyes grow wide. "That's it! My laptop is missing, too. I can't find the charger for my tablet, either. He's got it all in the car. He must! I've looked everywhere."

Vee drops her head into her hands. "This is it! If I don't

Snap Gwynneth by ten tonight, the Snapstreak will end. We've lost. No BBD for us."

All three of us sigh at the same time. All our big plans are doomed. The end. There's just no way it can happen now. "Joe the drummer is so cute, too," Megan says sadly.

Vee suddenly slaps her hand over her mouth and stands. She races out of the room and we hear loud barfing sounds coming out of the hallway bathroom. "Poor Vee," Megan says. "She looks terrible. We should say bye and let her rest. It's probably good she can't find her phone."

"I get what you're saying," I reply. "But no BBD? No Joe the drummer?"

Megan shrugs. "There's nothing we can do about it."

"I'd better check on Vee," I say. She's not in the bathroom, so I go to her bedroom. Vee is sprawled across her bed snoring loudly. I spread her quilt over her. She shouldn't be worrying over this Snapstreak stuff. That's easy enough to see.

That night Mom makes us soy burgers. We're eating them when the phone rings. "Hi Tom," Mom answers her phone. "How's Vee?"

Vee's dad! Suddenly I can't swallow. Is he calling to complain that we Snapped Vee? Has he looked at her phone and seen the video? Am I in trouble with Mom now?

"Yeah, I know what you mean," Mom says. "Of course you're welcome to borrow the book. It's the most clearly written book on kids' health that I've ever found. Hopefully Lulu will stay healthy and I won't need it for a while."

They're talking about a book. Whew! At least I'm not in trouble.

Mom gets off the call and gets up from the table. "Vee's dad is stopping by. He wants to read up on concussions, and I have a good medical book I was telling him about. He'll be here in a little while."

"You seem to be talking to him a lot these days," I say.

"Yes, I guess so," Mom says as she leaves the kitchen. I think she was blushing!

It hits me . . . like a bomb! Mom likes Vee's dad. Likes him like that! OMG!

As I eat, I wonder what it would be like to have Vee's dad as a stepdad. He seems pretty nice. Of course, Eric's a pest, but he's not the worst kid I've ever seen. I know it's early to have Mom and Tom married. Still . . . it could happen. Imagine me and Vee as sisters. Very cool.

When Tom arrives to pick up the book, I see that dark circles ring his eyes and that his right eye is twitching.

"Hey Lulu," he says.

"Hi."

Mom comes in holding a fat book. She's put on lipstick and brushed her hair. "Can I offer you a cup of tea?" Mom asks.

"Thanks, but I should get back to Vee. I'm so worried about her. She's sleeping now, so I figured it would be all right to run out for a little while."

"It'll just take a few minutes," Mom says. "Have you eaten?"

He says he hasn't, so Mom persuades him to have a soy burger and a cup of tea. "Just real quick."

While they eat, I sit on the couch to read the end of *The Witch of Blackbird Pond*, which I need to finish for ELA tomorrow. Although I'm into the book, I'm also kind of eavesdropping at the same time. I can't hear every word they're saying; their voices are lost among the clanking dishes, so I pay more attention to my book until I hear them step out in the hall again and I look up. "Vee doesn't understand how serious this is," Tom says to Mom. "I'd better get back. I don't want to leave her too long. Eric says he'll call if she needs me."

"I completely understand," Mom says.

A phone rings, and Tom reaches into the inside pocket of his sports jacket. "Hello?" The phone continues to ring, even though he's answered it. "Hello?"

There doesn't seem to be anyone on the other end and yet the phone is still ringing.

"This is Vee's phone," he says with a laugh as he suddenly realizes his mistake. "I forgot I even put it in my pocket. I meant to leave it in the trunk of the car." He grabs another phone from his outside jacket pocket. It's stopped ringing but he checks the caller ID. "It was Eric. I'd better get home," he says, hurrying toward the door. "Thanks for the burger, Susan." Mom hurries out the door behind him.

I hope Vee is all right. I wish I could text her, but there's no way to get in touch with her. I return to my book. After a while Mom comes in. She goes to the kitchen. Dishes clank and I get off the couch to help her. That's when I see it.

Tom put Vee's phone down on the hall table.

Will he miss it? Will he come right back searching for it? He was pretty distracted.

I press the home button on Vee's phone and see she has three new Snaps. Putting my hand over the screen, I whisk the phone into my back pocket. Maybe we're not out of the contest yet.

CHAPTER 14

VEE

MY HEAD HURTS. And my stomach. I hate feeling like this.

Dad rushes into my bedroom. "Eric says you've been crying. What's wrong?"

"I need my phone," I say.

Dad folds his arms angrily.

"And I feel terrible."

Dad puts his arm around me. "Forget it, kiddo. All your stuff is safe and sound."

"But you don't understand, Dad," I say.

"You're right. I don't understand. I don't care, either. All I care about is you getting well. It's late. Get to sleep," Dad says.

"Dad?" I ask as I get under the covers. "Did Lulu's mom ask if I could live with them?"

"What? No! Do you want to live with them?"

"I don't want to move," I tell him. It occurs to me that maybe I've hurt his feelings and I feel bad about that. "I would miss you, but it wouldn't be forever."

"Go to sleep," he says. "We'll talk in the morning. But forget it. You're not living with Lulu."

I lie in bed but I don't fall asleep right away. I realize that I'm happy he said no to me living with Lulu. It's nothing against Lulu. It's just good to know that he wouldn't let go of me so easily. I'm a little surprised that I feel this way. But I do.

Gwynneth must be wondering where I am. She's worrying that I'm not answering her on purpose. Maybe she thinks she sent a Snap that I didn't like. That I'm angry with her. I don't even know what she sent. I haven't been able to see it.

Why did this have to happen to me?! It's not fair!

If I'm not living with Lulu, then I'm definitely attending Shoreham Middle in a month's time. And Gwynneth—the coolest kid, the Queen Bee, GQB2the2ndpwr—will hate me by then for ignoring her and ruining her school's chance for a free Boys Being Dudes concert.

Now, not only will I be the new kid—I'll be the despised new kid. I'm sure Gwynneth will tell everybody what a loser I am.

Grabbing my pillow, I put it over my face. I want to hide from the world!

Wait! I'm already hiding from the world.

Now my head hurts even worse. Plus, here comes that twisty feeling in my stomach again. Where did I put that trash can? I'm going to puke.

CHAPTER 15

LULU CHATS WITH ME around nine.

Luloony

You'll never guess what just happened.

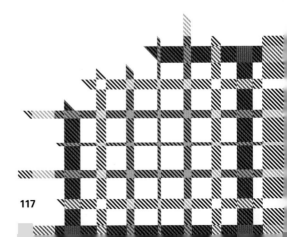

Megawatt

Lulu sends me a Snap video of herself joyfully dancing all around her room holding a phone in the air. I don't get it. How can she be holding her phone and also making a video at the same time?

Megawatt

Whose phone is that?

Luloony

vvvvvvvvvvvvvvvvvvvvvvvvvvvvvvvvvvvvvvv
vvvvvvvvvvv!!

Megawatt

 No!!!!!!!!!!!!!!!! How?

Luloony

I'll tell you tmrw. The hourglass is up. Have to send GQB2the2ndpwr a Snap right away.

Megawatt

What are you going to say?

Luloony

I hope your town falls into a sinkhole.

Megawatt

No! No! No! You can't!

Luloony

Lulu is just wild enough to really do it, so I'm relieved that it's a joke.

Megawatt

> See you tomorrow. Snap something nice to GQB2the2ndpwr

Luloony

> Later

I can't believe she got hold of Vee's phone. How could she have done it? This changes everything. We still have a chance. I imagine Joe the drummer waving to me from behind his drum set.

CHAPTER 16

I HAVE LOTS of pictures of Vee in my phone. I click on one where Megan, Vee, and I are making kissy faces at the phone camera and send it to Vee's phone. I doodle a message.

Wait! Gwynneth might know Vee's handwriting by now. I erase that and put in a banner that says BFFS FOR-EVER. Little fairies hold it on either side. Then I decide that the fairies might be too little-girlish. I switch the ban-ner carriers for bees. GQB2the2ndpwr isn't the only one who can have a hive. Let her think Vee is a Queen Bee in her own school.

Perfect, I think as I hit Send. I was in such a hurry to send out this Snap that I didn't even bother to read what Gwynneth sent. Who cares?

The important thing is to keep the Snapstreak going.

"Does Vee know you have her phone?" Megan asks the next day as soon as she gets on the bus.

"How would she know?" I ask. "There's no way to get in touch with her."

"Do they have a landline?" Megan asks.

A landline? Is she kidding? "Do those even exist anymore?" I ask.

"We have one . . . I think," Megan says. "Mom says in case there's a storm or a national emergency she wants a landline."

"If Vee has a landline I have no idea what the number is," I say. "Do you?"

"No," Megan replies. "I guess we'll just have to go over there this afternoon."

Vee's phone rings and I dig it out of my backpack. She got a Snap from a baby friend. I'm surprised that Gwynneth is still coming up as a baby after all this time. But it isn't Gwynneth! "Ethan Myers," I tell Megan quietly. He's a baby, so they must have just started Snapping. Maybe he's been checking to see how she feels.

Megan's eyes grow wide. "Should we look?"

"Of course!"

"Isn't it sort of an intrusion on Vee's privacy?" Megan asks. "A very, very, very big intrusion."

Megan and I look at each other. I don't know. Is it? "What if we don't answer and he thinks Vee is ignoring him?" I say.

"It wouldn't hurt to take a peek," Megan says.

"Just a peek," I agree. How can we not? Holding Vee's phone low, we open Ethan's Snap. It's a video. He's filmed a bunch of fish! Tropical fish!

Ethan 🤍 🤍

> My mom says someone with a concussion should
> only do restful things. These fish seem pretty tranquil
> so I hope you like fish . . .

"That is so sweet!" Megan says. "Oh, I love it!"

"I can't believe he knows a word like *tranquil!*" I say.

"Fish are restful," Megan says. Suddenly she looks panicked. "This video is going to disappear before we get a chance to show Vee. She'll never know Ethan sent it."

"We'll just tell her about it," I say.

"But then she'll know we watched it," Megan says. "We'll just have to confess."

"You're right," I agree. As we roll along toward school, though, I imagine how it will be this afternoon when we visit Vee and tell her we have her phone. The first thing she's going to say is, "Let me have it." She's not going to take no for an answer, either.

It's as though Megan has been reading my mind, because the next thing she says is "Vee's going to want her phone back, isn't she?"

I nod. "Yes, she is."

"It would be bad for her health if we gave her back her phone, wouldn't it?"

Of course, the answer is yes! It would be very bad! But I don't want to lie to Vee. I've never lied to Vee about anything in my entire life.

"She might not like us taking over her Snapstreak,"

Megan says. "But what if we give her back her phone and she gets sicker because she's Snapping with Gwynneth—and now Ethan? And you know she'd start Snapping with us and we'd Snap back because we couldn't ignore her. You know we just couldn't. Then she wouldn't get better and it would be all our fault. What kind of friends would we be then? The worst! The worst! The worst!"

Megan definitely made sense. "But how can we not tell her?"

"I don't know," Megan says. "What should we do? I have no idea."

"That makes two of us," I say.

By the time we get to Vee's house that afternoon, Megan and I still haven't figured out what we're going to tell her. When Eric answers the door he tells us that Vee's sleeping. We turn to leave but she appears on the stairs. "Don't go!" she says. "I'm awake."

Barely. Her eyes are puffy and her hair looks like she stuck her finger in an electrical socket. She's got on yellow pajamas with a pattern of kittens playing with balls of yarn. They're way too big for her. I've never even seen them before and I've slept over at her house plenty. Vee sees me staring at her pajamas and laughs lightly. "My grandma sent me these when she heard I was sick," she says, smiling down at them. "I barfed on everything else I usually wear to bed."

"I think they're adorable," Megan says.

"They're very special," I say.

Vee rolls her eyes because she knows I'm messing with her. "Come on up to my bedroom," she says. Vee's room is always neat but today it's a mess. The sheets and blankets are tossed into a knot. Her wastebasket overflows with tissues, and, to be honest, there's a kind of barfy smell. Megan immediately starts smoothing out the blankets. "Get back into bed," she tells Vee. "We have some things to tell you."

Thank goodness Megan's taking the lead on this because, honestly, I had no idea what to do.

Vee's face grows serious. "Something bad?"

"No," Megan says. "It's all good. Good. Good. Good."

"Good," Vee says.

"Exactly," Megan says. "It's just that we want you to stay calm when you hear our news. Promise?"

"How can I promise when I don't know what the news is?" Vee asks.

"You have to promise or we won't tell you," Megan says.

"Aw, come on!" Vee says. "That's not fair!"

"Just promise!" I say, growing impatient.

"All right. I promise," Vee says.

Megan turns toward me. "Lulu, tell Vee how you got hold of her phone."

"YOU HAVE MY PHONE!!!" Vee cries out. Actually, it's more like a scream.

"Vee, remember that you're still getting better. You promised to stay calm. It's important for you to get better," Megan reminds Vee. "Let Lulu talk."

Vee presses her hands over her mouth so she won't say anything as I tell the story of how her dad mistakenly picked up her phone when Eric was calling him on his own phone, which was in his other pocket. "He was so worried about you that he put your phone down on a hall table and rushed out of the house without taking it."

"Has he mentioned it?" Megan asks. "Does he realize he's forgotten it?"

Vee shakes her head. "He told me all my stuff was in his car and then he took it to work so there was no chance I'd find it. He's totally forgotten he had it in his pocket that day. He thinks it's with the other stuff."

"Excellent!" I say.

"The Snapstreak is already broken, though, isn't it?"

"I sent Gwynneth a Snap from your phone last night," I tell Vee.

"Great! Did she reply?"

"Not yet," I say.

"Okay. I'll have to wait for her reply. Can I have my phone?" Vee asks.

I'm not kidding when I say that Vee actually gets a sparkle in her eyes now that she thinks she's getting her phone back. Megan sees it, too, and shoots me a worried look. "Here's the thing," Megan begins. "We don't think it would be good for you if we gave you your phone."

There it is. It's out. Megan squeezes her hands into two fists as she waits for the explosion. I chew lightly on my lower lip, also expecting Vee to blow.

"I suppose you're right," Vee says.

Megan and I stare at each other in complete disbelief. Did she really just say that?!

We must look completely shocked because Vee laughs. "I mean it. I know you're right. Dad took me to a doctor this morning and she told me all the bad stuff that can happen if I don't let my brain rest," Vee says. "She showed me pictures of swollen brains and brains of athletes who have had lots of untreated concussions. It was scary. I want to get better from this."

Megan eases Vee back down onto her pillow. "Okay, you rest, remember? Vee and I will keep the Snapstreak going. We can handle it. There's absolutely nothing for you to worry about. We've got this. Totally got it."

"We still have to discuss the fish," I say, wishing we didn't have to.

Vee looks confused. "Fish?"

Megan tells her about the aquarium Snap from Ethan. Vee gets all soft and dreamy-eyed. "Can I just see it for a second?"

"No," Megan says. "It disappeared. Besides, you can't be on the phone."

Vee's eyes narrow as she realizes something. "Hey, this means you guys will be reading all my email, texts, tweets, Facebook messages, and Instagram."

"We'll answer Ethan and just say thanks and you appreciate it and hope he's well," Megan says.

"All right," Vee agrees. "I'm not sure how I feel about this."

"You show us everything anyway," I say with a shrug.

"That's true," Vee agrees. "But don't you guys write anything that makes me look like an idiot, okay?"

"We'd never do that," Megan says.

"I'm trusting you with my phone," Vee says.

"We'll guard it with our lives," I say. I mean it when I say it, too. At that moment, I have no idea that things are going to get so crazy.

CHAPTER 17

BEING CUT OFF from the Internet plays tricks with my mind. It's as though there's a whole world going on and I can't be any part of it. I might as well have washed up on a desert island. It's lonely, too. Out there kids are sending each other funny stuff. They're talking about what's going on in their lives, in school, on TV. And here I am. Alone. Doing nothing.

I'm not even allowed to read a book. Here's what I'm allowed to do: knit! I'm not kidding. My grandma taught me to knit and the doctor said that would be all right as long as I don't strain my eyes knitting for hours on end. As if! But it's better than nothing, so I drag out my old, tangled yarn and the half-done scarf I abandoned because it was getting way wider than I'd planned. And I knit.

While I knit, I stare out the window. Heidi Dog comes to see me and I scoop her up onto the bed. I think she knows I'm sick because she snuggles up closer than usual next to me. Out the window I see our neighbor's black and white cat stalk a pair of cardinals feeding in the grass. They don't seem to notice the cat. They're in trouble and they don't even know it. I rap hard on the window and they fly away. The cat glares angrily. He doesn't know it was me who's spoiled his hunt.

I worry. About everything. What crazy stuff are Megan and Lulu sending to Gwynneth? They wouldn't intentionally make me seem strange, but . . . in their own way, each of them has a unique approach to the world. Just different from mine. Will what they send seem like it comes from me? Giving my phone to them—to anyone, really—is much harder than I would have expected.

Heidi Dog leaves my side. I assume she's heading to her doggie door to do her business out in the yard. That gives me the idea to walk her. I haven't walked her since last summer vacation. The doctor said I could go outside as long as I don't overdo it.

It takes a bit of searching to find her leash, but I find it on a coat hook, and soon we're outside in the beautiful day. I love spring, not only because school's almost over but also because the winter always seems so long to me. Heidi Dog wags her tail and seems glad to be out seeing different things.

I've always lived in this same neighborhood. It's a little on the dull side and it never occurred to me that I would miss it if I had to leave. But now that I'll be going, it suddenly seems like the nicest place on earth. I know most of my neighbors. What I used to think was boring now is familiar and comforting.

When we turn the corner, I see Ethan standing in his front yard, three doors down. He should be in school.

Uh-oh! I stop. Did I brush my hair? Have I brushed my teeth? Deodorant? I've become such a slug these last few days I can't remember. What am I even wearing? Sweatpants and this old T-shirt with the bleach stains.

As I take one step back, Heidi Dog barks. She wants to go forward. Ethan turns toward the sound. His face lights with surprise and he waves, swinging his arm in a wide arc. Waving back, I step forward. There's no chance of retreat now.

I hope Ethan really likes me for myself, because he's about to get a super dose of the real me.

"Hey!" he says, smiling as I approach. "Why are you walking around? Aren't you supposed to be resting?"

"Resting my mind," I say. "Aren't you supposed to be in school?"

"I woke up this morning and my stomach hurt. At the

time I thought I was dying but now I feel better. Maybe it was something I ate." He looks at me and I don't see any signs of horror or even disgust. Maybe I don't look as horrible as I thought. I start to relax.

"Cute dog," Ethan says as he reaches down to scratch Heidi Dog between the ears.

"Do you have a dog?" I ask.

"No. A cat. She's around here somewhere. I came out to look for her because she's got to go to the vet when my mom comes home from work."

"Is she all right?"

"Yeah. Just a checkup." He looks around and calls for Fluffy. "My little sister named her," he explains.

"My brother, Eric, named Heidi Dog."

We talk about our pets for a while and laugh about the funny things they do sometimes. I'm having such a nice time talking with Ethan that I let Heidi Dog off the leash so she can wander around a little while we chat. I have gloves and a plastic bag to scoop her poop if she goes on someone's lawn.

Talking to Ethan is surprisingly easy. I thank him for his fish Snap. He looks away shyly. "It was sort of dumb, I guess," he says.

"No!" I say. "I liked it a lot."

"Really?" He smiles.

"Yes! It was totally cute."

He asks me if my Snapstreak is still going and I tell

him about how Lulu and Megan have taken over. "Does the girl you're Snapping with know it's not you?" Ethan asks.

"Not yet. Do you think it still counts as a streak if it's not me?"

"I don't know," Ethan says. "I guess so. It's still a streak between the same two users. Maybe you should tell the girl. What's her name?"

"Gwynneth. She goes to Shoreham Middle School."

"My cousin Jack goes there."

"Does he like it?" I ask.

"I think so."

Suddenly I hear a horrible screech. Fluffy and Heidi Dog have met. Fluffy is a ball of terrified white fur. Heidi Dog is so scared that she runs under the front steps of Ethan's house. "Fluffy! Stop!" Ethan scolds.

"Heidi Dog! It's all right," I say as I sit next to the stairs. "Come on out." The poor dog just shivers with fear.

Ethan picks up Fluffy and carries her into the house. He comes back out with something in his hand. He kneels down beside me and offers the treats in his palm. "Here, Heidi Dog," he says, holding out some string cheese. "Come get it. That bad old Fluffy is in the house."

He definitely has Heidi Dog's attention and she slowly makes her way out, gobbling the cheese from Ethan's hand. When she's done she stretches up to lick Ethan's cheek. "She likes you," I say.

"Animals always like you when you feed them," he says, laughing. He's extra cute when he smiles. And I like his laugh. "Listen," he says. "When you win this free concert by BBD."

"If I win," I say. "If we win."

"I have faith. You'll win. We'll win. Everyone says so."

What is he asking me? Is this a date? I need to be sure. "Me and you?"

He laughs his nice laugh. "Yeah. My mom could drive us."

"Sure," I say. My heart is racing but I try to act calm.

"I mean . . . we don't have to wait for the concert," he says. "Once you feel better we could do something else together. I was going to ask you but then you got hit in the head."

"Bad timing." My throat is getting dry. "But I'll get better . . . eventually."

"Sure you will!" We smile at each other. We probably look pretty goofy—standing there grinning like two idiots—but I couldn't care less. It feels wonderful!

CHAPTER 18

HAVING SOMEONE ELSE'S phone is a huge responsibility. In school, Lulu and I take turns checking it. We don't want to miss anything Gwynneth might send through. I get caught checking it during ELA. Ms. Harris, our teacher, gives me a hard stare. Quick, quick, quick, I stash it in my backpack. My parents will be super mad if I get sent to SAP again.

At lunch on Tuesday, Lulu and I check the phone under the table. Nothing. That's what we're doing when the big TV at the front of the lunchroom comes on. Looking out the window, I see that it's started to rain. They only turn on the big TV when we won't be going out after lunch.

The TV is set to Channel 14 and the local news is on. There are a lot of stories about people being hit by cars, trees falling down in high winds, and the new bridge they're building. None of it is all that interesting to Lulu and me (or any of the other kids, either), but when Heather May appears on screen, our eyeballs are instantly glued to the screen because the first thing she says is: "Heather May here with an update on our Channel 14 Snapstreak contest."

"We have some front-runners. We interviewed the girl currently in the number-one spot, Mathlete Gwynneth Plotkin, from Shoreham Middle School in Shoreham."

Lulu and I stare at each other, wide-eyed. "Gwynneth! A Mathlete?!" we say at the same moment. Gwynneth comes on, standing in front of Shoreham High beside Heather May. "Is it difficult to keep your Snapstreak going, Gwynneth?" Heather May asks.

Gwynneth seems nervous, which is not how I've pictured her. Vee had us thinking that Gwynneth was the coolest thing on two feet. She's wearing that heavy eye makeup, though, and her hair is up in a ponytail, which is how Vee described her. "Who are you Snapstreaking with?" Heather May asks.

"Oh, just a friend from another school," Gwynneth replies.

"Just a friend?!" Lulu cries out. Everyone in the cafeteria turns to look at her. Lulu stands up, looking angry, and shouts up at the TV screen. "That friend is Olivia Howard, Gwynneth. You could at least mention her name."

Mrs. Ross, one of the lunch monitors, hurries over and puts her hand on Lulu's shoulder. "Stay calm, Lulu," she says. "Another outburst like that could get you sent to SAP."

Lulu sits. "She could have at least mentioned Vee's name," Lulu repeats more quietly.

The lunchroom buzzes with kids chattering. Thanks to Lulu's outburst, they all know that Vee is the one who has been Snapping with Gwynneth.

"Vee is Snapping with this girl, Gwynneth! Awesome!" says a girl named Madison.

"We don't know," I say in a small voice. It's so obviously a lie!

"But Vee is hurt," Madison says. "She can't keep it up."

"She can," I say.

"We have to help her," another girl named Emma says. "We have to win that concert. She's our only hope." Other kids have started to gather around, curious about what's going on.

"I heard Vee needs to rest," a third girl named Bella says. "What if she sleeps through Gwynneth's Snap?"

"If she breaks the streak we won't get to see Boys Being Dudes!" a boy named Carl shouts.

The TV snaps off. Mrs. Ross and two other lunch monitors hurry around telling everyone to calm down.

They threaten to send the whole lunchroom full of kids to SAP. (What a crazy scene that would be!)

"Whatever you do, don't let anyone know we have Vee's phone," Lulu whispers to me when the other kids have gone back to their own tables.

"You're right," I agree. "It could get crazy."

That night I feel all restless and uneasy. Lulu takes Vee's phone with her, so I can't even check if Gwynneth is sending anything. It's making me anxious.

Some fan-fiction writing might help calm me. I write that Bilbo is on his quest along with his best friend, Sam, when a wicked fairy named Gwynmoth appears. She gets Bilbo and Sam to drag a boat across a goopy bog for her. When the wizard, Gandalf, appears and asks who performed this amazing feat, Gwynmoth says, "Oh, just a friend from another shire."

"That's right, Gwynmoth, hog all the glory for yourself, why don't you?" Sam shouts.

Bilbo doesn't say anything but decides that he doesn't like Gwynmoth one bit.

Writing this was fun but it didn't really calm me down. Lulu would text me if Gwynneth Snapped her, wouldn't she? I can't stand not knowing anymore. I have to find out.

CHAPTER 19

VEE'S DAD COMES over again tonight after supper to return Mom's book. He and Mom sit out on the screened back porch, talking. It's nice to see Mom smile so much. Except, I'm having a nervous meltdown. I'm just waiting for Vee's dad to say, "By the way, Susan, did I happen to leave Vee's phone here the other evening?"

I lurk around, waiting for it to happen, trying desperately to come up with some believable denial. "No, I'm sure you didn't. I would have seen it." Or, "Didn't you say all that stuff was in your office?"

Mom definitely realizes I'm not acting normally. "Is there something you need, Lulu?" Mom asks while I'm pretending to look through some old magazines stacked on the porch.

"No," I say. "Just looking for something to read."

"Would you like to join us?" Vee's dad asks.

"No thanks."

At that second, Vee's phone rings. It's in my backpack somewhere in another room. My heart skips a beat. I thought I'd turned it off. I recognize the ringtone immediately.

"Vee uses that same ringtone," her dad says.

"Does she?" I ask, my voice going all shrill. OMG! OMG! He's going to figure it out any second!

"Yes, the exact same one," Vee's dad says.

"Us kids love that one the best," I say, talking too fast. "Nearly all of us use the same one. That's definitely my phone."

"I never heard you use that ringtone before," Mom says.

"I just put it on the phone the other day."

"Well, are you going to answer it?" Mom asks.

"Yes! Sure!" I hurry out of the room and, of course, I can't find my backpack . . . ANYWHERE!!!! I run around everywhere looking for it, like a lunatic. And all the while it rings, rings, rings, rings, and rings. With every ring I'm POSITIVE Vee's dad will remember that he left the phone here.

Naturally, when I finally find the backpack, Vee's phone stops ringing. The caller ID tells me it was Megan calling. Why is she calling me on Vee's phone? I'm about to call her back when I see a new Snap pop up. It's from Gwynneth.

I was nervous

It's no fun getting back at Gwynneth if she's already sorry.

I go to my camera roll and select a photo of Vee, Megan, and me. "Sorry isn't good enough. I have real friends," I write on the photo.

I remember a time when I was in the sixth grade. I went to see a play with Mom and afterward a reporter stepped up to us with a microphone and asked how we had liked it. I looked away and couldn't even speak. I completely froze.

I change the writing.

My friends and I say good job 👍

I hit Send.

💬

The next day it rains heavily. That little uncovered patch between the bus and the front door was enough to totally soak me. The maintenance staff is mopping like crazy, trying to keep the floors dry, but it's no use. All I want is to get to my locker, dry my hair on a paper towel, and pull off my soaked sweater.

I'm not prepared to see a crowd of kids waiting at my locker, dripping all over the floor. This is very peculiar.

What could they want? Those girls Emma, Bella, and Madison are at the center of things. "'Sup?" I ask as I twirl my combination lock.

Madison smiles at me brightly. "We're here to help."

"Thanks, but unless you have towels there's not much you can do," I say.

Megan comes around the corner. Her eyes go wide when she sees so many kids surrounding me. "They want to help with Vee's Snapstreak," I explain.

Megan freezes, recovers, and says, "But we don't have Vee's phone. Right, Lulu?"

"Right." I say, hoping they believe us.

"You guys must be helping Vee—there's no way she could keep the Snapstreak going in her condition. We want to help," Madison says.

"How about you keep hold of it and we take turns Snapping at lunchtime?" Emma says. The crowd of kids murmur their agreement with that idea. They seem to think it would work.

"We can try it, I suppose," I say to Megan.

She shrugs. "I guess so."

"Great! We'll meet you at lunchtime," Bella says.

"I don't like this," Megan says when they leave.

"Same here," I say. "It's just going to get crazy. Who knows what these kids are going to Snap?"

"At lunch I'll tell them to forget it," I say.

"Good idea," Megan says. "I'll stay right with you in case Madison, Bella, and Emma argue with you."

"Thanks."

"You're welcome," Megan says. She turns—and then spins backward, her arms windmilling, and slides into a bank of lockers.

I plead to be allowed to ride in the ambulance with Megan, the nurse, and the EMT. The nurse calls my mom to check if it's okay and, thank goodness, she says yes. I try to comfort Megan as she whimpers and cries. Even though the EMT gives her some medicine, I can see that Megan's in a lot of pain.

Once she gets out of the x-ray room, they know for sure that her left arm is broken. They set it in a cast. "Can I sign it?" I ask the nurse.

"Sure," she says, and hands me a marker.

Megan's mom met us at the hospital and by the time Megan is released it's the last period of the day. "I might as well bring you home," she says, and she drops me in front of my house.

"I'll call you in a few to see how you're doing," I say as I scoot out of the backseat.

"Thanks," she says with a weak little smile. I can

tell she's still in pain. "You'll have to do the Snap again tonight," Megan adds.

"No problem," I say. "Feel better."

"Hurry," Megan's mom says. "You're getting soaked."

Splashing through puddles, I reach the front door—and then suddenly I stop short. Vee's phone! It's in my backpack, which I left in my locker. By the time Mom gets home from work to drive me back to school, it will be locked up tight.

No phone, no Snapstreak.

CHAPTER 20

SUDDENLY I DON'T mind resting my brain. All I want to do is think about Ethan, and that doesn't involve written words, keyboards, or lit-up screens. All I have to do is close my eyes to picture his wonderful smile. I've liked him for a while now, but now that I know—for sure—that he likes me back . . . I'm just so happy about it.

Ethan can't call, text, email, or Snapchat with me. It's all for a great cause, though. I'm now totally determined to get better. I imagine Ethan and me side by side at the BBD concert. It's going to be great!

Dad comes in and sits at the edge of my bed. "How are you feeling?"

"My head hurts, but not as bad as before. I didn't puke at all today."

"It sounds as if you're improving. That's great," he says.

"When can I go back to school?" I ask.

"The doctor wants you to give it three weeks, so maybe after next week. I called her today and she said you can start catching up on homework if you feel up to it."

"I'll need my laptop," I say. "And my phone."

"Let's wait until next week to see how you're doing and we can talk about it."

I nod. Truthfully I'm still a bit more tired than usual. Just taking that walk around the neighborhood with Heidi Dog wore me out. I slept for two hours when I got home. It's possible that I wouldn't have been able to keep up with the Snapstreak. I'm glad Megan and Lulu are taking care of it.

"Dad, are we moving next week?" I ask. I haven't seen any packing going on.

Dad shakes his head. "I had to pass on that offer. We can't move until you get better."

This is excellent news. It means I'll graduate from the eighth grade with my class.

"Are you hungry?" Dad asks. "I brought home some burgers."

Getting out of bed, I follow Dad out of the room. I have a happy feeling inside. Dad has postponed the move, Ethan asked me out, and my Snapstreak with Gwynneth is in good hands.

CHAPTER 21

OMG! OMG! OMG! I ride my bike all the way to school in the pouring rain. I finally get there, totally DRENCHED. But at least I'm there. Leaning my bike against the school, I yank on the glass doors at the front. LOCKED!!!!!!!!!!

A streak of lightning crackles and then thunder. This storm is right on top of us. I splash through puddles around to the side door. Also locked. BANG! BANG! BANG! "Anybody there? Let me in!" BANG! BANG! BANG!

I see through the glass that there's a classroom with its door open and a light on. After more banging, Mr. Sweeney, a seventh grade social studies teacher, steps out and walks to the door. He lets me in. "Lulu, you're soaked. What's wrong?"

"I left my backpack in my locker. Thanks for opening up."

"What's in there that's so important?" he asks.

"Believe me, it's important," I say as I trudge down the hall, trailing a stream of rainwater behind me. "It's more important than you can imagine."

As I'm taking my backpack out of my locker, Madison and Bella walk by. They stop by my locker. "What happened to you, Lulu?" Madison asks. "How did you get so wet?"

"I rode my bike here," I tell them.

"Why would you do that?" Bella asks.

"I felt like it," I say, sounding as annoyed as I feel. Why are they so nosy? "Why are you two here?"

"Pep club," they answer at the same time.

"How's Megan?" Bella asks. "We heard she slipped on the wet floor."

"She broke her arm." They both gasp and say how terrible they feel. They're okay girls, really. Not exactly my type, but okay anyway.

"You didn't leave Vee's phone in that backpack, did you?" Madison asks.

"Maybe," I say.

"You'd better check it," Bella says, sounding worried. "What if Gwynneth sent a Snap?"

There would still be time to answer it. To make them happy, though, I take the phone out of my pack to check it.

"Don't get that phone wet," Madison says. "That's

an extremely valuable phone." Annoying as that is, she's right. "Let me check," Madison says, lifting the phone from my hand. She dries it on her sleeve before turning it on. "There's a Snap here from Ethan Myers," Madison says, sounding impressed. She looks to Bella, her eyebrows raised meaningfully. "Ethan Myers."

Bella nods. "Ethan Myers," she says. "Wow!" Ethan Myers might be happy to know he's so well approved of. Vee will also be thrilled to hear that he sent her a Snap.

"But nothing from Gwynneth," Madison reports. She slips the phone into the Boys Being Dudes tote bag she has slung over her shoulder. "You'd better let me take charge of this for now. If you get moisture in there, you could ruin the phone. And then where would we all be? Nowhere, that's where. Snapstreak broken. Pfft! Just like that. Over and out. No BBD for any of us. You'd better go home to dry off. I'll give it back to you tomorrow. Don't worry. I'll keep the Snapstreak going until then."

It all happened so fast. One minute I had Vee's phone in my dripping-wet hand—and the next Madison and Bella were trotting off with it.

Why didn't I run after them to demand they return the phone?

I guess in my heart I thought Madison might be right. I've ruined more than one phone by getting it wet. Once, I had it in my back jeans pocket. When I got up from the toilet, plunk! It fell right in. I tried to use the blow dryer on it. I even stuck it in a bowl of rice like they tell you to—nothing. Another time I was out on a friend's boat. A Jet Ski went by and sprayed us all just as I was calling Mom to tell her I'd be late. That phone went kaput, too. And she did say she'd return Vee's phone to me tomorrow.

💬

The only thing is, the next day I'm really sick. I mean, I can hardly lift my head off the pillow sick. I'm burning hot, and my throat feels like someone is shooting off a flamethrower inside of it. "I'll bet you picked up some germ in the hospital," Mom says. Being out in the wet, cold rain couldn't have helped, either. Megan calls me but I feel too awful to even answer.

I guess I should be happy that Madison has the phone. Neither Megan nor I are able to do much with it now. Still, weak as I am, I can't stop worrying. I can't quite believe that things have gotten so out of control.

CHAPTER 22

THERE'S NO REAL reason that I need to stay home from school the next day. I'm left-handed, so I'm not going to be able to write or type, not in a way anyone else will be able to read. Still I should go, I guess.

When I get on the bus, Lulu isn't there. I text her, using my right thumb as best I can. "U OK?" Everyone is interested in signing my cast, so the bus ride is fun, fun, fun, and the time flies by. Before I know it, we're almost at the school and I still haven't heard back from Lulu. I figure I'd better call, which I do, but the call goes right to voicemail.

I'm nearly at my locker when my phone buzzes.

> **Lulu: You have to get Vee's phone. I'm sick.**

"I THrB U IT," I type. It's the best I can do one-handed. Autocorrect changes it to "I throw bats."

Somehow Lulu guesses what I mean.

> **Lulu: Will explain later. Madison has it.**

Madison has it?! What? How did that happen?

"IWLLGFRAMHR," I type, which is as close to "I will get it from her" as I can manage. Autocorrect changes it to "I'll willingly frame her."

This time Lulu doesn't guess correctly.

> **Lulu: Tie her up with a bow while you're at it.**

Madison isn't on my bus, so I set out to find her as soon I get into school. This isn't that easy because everyone wants to sign my cast. By the time the buzzer for the start of first period sounds, I still haven't seen Madison. At the end of first period, on my way to my second class, pre-algebra, I see her friend Emma and hurry up behind her.

"Hey, Emma. Have you seen Madison?" I ask.

"She has a dentist appointment this morning," Emma says.

"Oh. Does she still have Vee's phone?"

"I think Bella has it," Emma tells me.

"Thanks," I say. I know Bella is in pre-algebra, so I don't worry too much. I stand by the classroom door waiting for her. "Hey, Bella, Emma says you have Vee's phone?"

"I did have it, but Maria Scelza wanted to send a Snap to Gwynneth so I let her take the phone."

"Did you hear from Gwynneth? Is the Snapstreak still going?" I ask, feeling a little bit panicky.

"Yep. Madison and I answered her last night. Can I sign your cast?"

Maria is in the seventh grade, so I'm not so sure where to find her, and we only have four minutes to get from one class to the next. After pre-algebra I have academic skills. I get a pass to the library, but instead of going, I walk around the school peeking in windows looking for Maria. As I'm peering into a science lab I sense a presence looming behind me. I turn and discover our assistant principal, Mr. McCarty, staring down at me. "What's going on, Megan?" he asks.

My mouth opens but no sound comes out.

"I'm waiting," Mr. McCarty says.

"I'm looking for Maria Scelza. She has Vee's phone," I reply. He doesn't smile, not even a blink, and I realize that this isn't as important to him as it is to me. "For the Snapstreak contest," I add. "For the school to win a free concert."

Nothing. He totally doesn't care.

"And where are you supposed to be?" he asks.

"The library."

"I'll walk with you to the SAP room," he says.

"Aw, please," I say. "My parents will be super mad at me. They told me no SAP for the rest of the year."

"You should have thought of that before you decided not to report to the library."

I point to my cast. "Don't you think I've suffered enough?" I'm desperate.

A flicker of a smile crosses his face and I have a moment of hope, but it doesn't last long. "Let's go," he says. The SAP room is on the other side of the school and it seems to take a hundred years to get there. Every so often some kids pass by and they look at me with big sympathetic eyes, like I'm a prisoner about to be sent to the gallows. Despite the misery of the situation, when I arrive at the SAP room, I have to smile.

Maria Scelza is there, too!

As soon as I sit, I pull a sheet from my spiral notebook. I want to ask her if she has Vee's phone. My right-handed writing is just scribble-scrabble though. Finally at the end of the period, I catch up with her at last. "I've been looking all over for you. I can't believe I found you in here," I say.

"It's all because of Vee's phone," she says. "I was checking it for a Gwynneth message and I got caught and sent to SAP."

This isn't good. "Who has it now?" I ask.

"I handed it to Emmett Maloney just before Ms. Pate sent me to SAP," Maria says.

"Where is Emmett Maloney now?"

"Band, I think."

Can I get to the band room and back to my next class, Spanish, in four minutes? I have to try. There's no running allowed in the halls, so I racewalk to the band room to wait for Emmett. When he shows up I practically pounce on him. "I need Vee's phone," I say. He looks at me like I'm nuts, which I can understand.

"Oh, I sent that Gwyn girl a video of Rae Gonzalez playing the tuba," Emmett says. "She got right back to me. She loved it."

"Great!" I say. The Snapstreak is still going. "Can I have the phone?"

"I gave it to somebody." He looks at the ceiling, thinking. "I don't remember who it was though."

"Think!" I say.

Again he gazes up. "I wasn't even looking. Someone's hand shot out for the phone and I just handed it off after I sent the video." He shrugs. "Hey, can I sign your cast?"

In Spanish we're conjugating irregular verbs, but I don't hear much of the lesson. Who could have that phone? How will I get it back? What would Bilbo Baggins do?

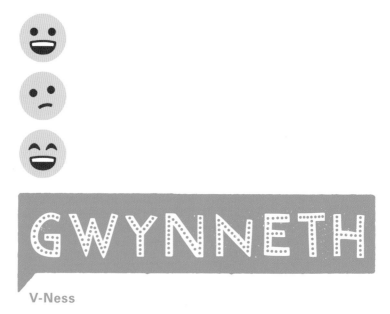

CHAPTER 23

GWYNNETH

V-Ness

Hi G! You looked gr8 on TV. My friends Madison, Bella, Emma and I love pep club. This is our pep club room.

GWYNNETH

GQB2the2ndpwr

You have so many friends! And you do so many activities. Here's our Mathlete trophy.

V-Ness

Hi Second Power. How do u like 8th gr?
I can't wait to get to 8th gr.

GQB2the2ndpwr

Aren't you in 8 now?

GQB2the2ndpwr

V-Ness

Oh yeah! I forgot. I'm V. Sure! I'm in 8.

GQB2the2ndpwr

Strange.

V-Ness

That's me. Strange.

GQB2the2ndpwr

Lol. How's this for strange?

V-Ness

Way strange! Lol!  it!!!!!!!!!!!!!!!!!!!
Is this your brother?

GQB2the2ndpwr

I didn't know you can draw, too. Wow! When did that happen? It does look a bit like my brother. Lol! Here's another strange one.

V-Ness

Here is a video of Rae Gonzalez playing the tuba.

GQB2the2ndpwr

 it!

V-Ness

Vee is a v nice girl. We all like her a lot.

V-Ness

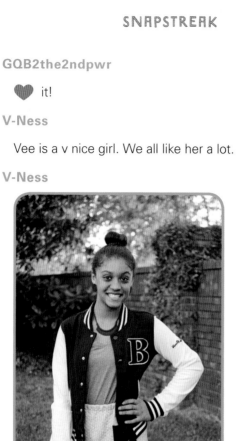

GQB2the2ndpwr

Wait! Isn't this V?!

V-Ness

No! It's Tony Ellis. Didn't you know Vee has a concussion? She can't use her phone.

GQB2the2ndpwr

Really? I once had a concussion too. It's the worst.

But if Vee hasn't been using her phone, who have I been talking to?

CHAPTER 24

YOU **LOST MY** phone?!" I cry out once it sinks in what Lulu and Megan have been trying to tell me. They stand at the end of my bed looking like they'd rather be anywhere else in the world.

"It's not actually lost, in fact," Lulu says. "Someone has it."

"We just don't know who," Megan adds. "Yet. We don't know yet."

"It keeps moving." Lulu sits at the edge of my bed. "And . . . sooner or later we will catch up with it."

"How long has it been gone?" I ask.

They look at each other guiltily. "About three days," Megan says in a little, squeaky voice.

"Three days! I can't believe you guys!" I shout. "I trusted you! I'm stuck here at home and now my phone is lost."

Megan steps closer to me. "You're not the only one having a hard time, you know," she says. "I broke my arm and Lulu's had a very high fever. Lulu rode her bike all the way to the school in the pouring rain to get the phone. And I got sent to SAP for the SECOND time because I was looking all over the place for that stupid phone, so I think you might want to give us a break."

When someone tells you you're acting like a jerk and you realize they're right, it's not the greatest feeling the world. So I don't answer Megan right away. There's an awkward silence. "If you know what I mean," Megan says, finally.

"Sorry," I say.

"We're sorry we lost track of your phone," Lulu says.

"We are," Megan agrees. "We never meant for it to happen. We kept thinking we were about to find it, but we never did."

The front doorbell rings. I figure Eric will get it, but when it rings again, I get out of bed and hurry down the stairs. I'm feeling a lot better. The doctor says I can go back to school, but not gym. Or sports. I can't risk getting hit on the head again. Plus less electronics. In bed by ten every night. It's not forever, just until they're sure my brain has healed.

I check the side window to see who's outside and I panic. Ethan!

Lulu and Megan are on the stairs. "Ethan," I whisper.

They race upstairs and instantly return with a hairbrush, lip gloss, and even a breath mint. "One second," I call as they frantically fix me up. It'll have to do. I don't want him to leave.

"Hi," I say cheerily, opening the door. Then my eyes go wide when I see what he's holding. "MY PHONE!" I cry out happily.

"HER PHONE!" Megan and Lulu cheer.

Smiling, he hands the phone to me, stepping inside the house. "I thought you'd be happy to get this."

"Happy is not the word!" I say. "How did you get it?"

"A kid at lunch handed it to me," he says. "When I saw it was yours, I just put it in my pocket."

"Thanks so much!" The first thing I check is the Snapstreak.

"It's still going!!!!!" I shout.

"She knows it's not you," Ethan says. "Apparently Tony Ellis came right out and told her. That didn't stop her, though. She kept answering."

"Good old Gwynneth," Lulu says. "What a trooper!"

"Wait a minute," I say, checking the calendar app on my phone. "Today is the last day!" I notice the hourglass. Only a half hour left!

V-Ness

GQB2the2ndpwr

CHAPTER 25

So WE FINALLY get to meet Gwynneth in person. She's not wearing all that eyeliner. "I was just trying something," she tells us. We're at the shared Pleasant Hill/ Shoreham Middle Schools Boys Being Dudes concert, standing in the lobby of the Shoreham High Performing Arts Center. The schools decided to hold the concert here since it's big and new. The place is PACKED because the tickets are cheap and everyone loves BBD.

"Why did we have to buy tickets if we won a free concert?" Megan asks.

"Did you forget? It's a fundraiser," Vee says. She and Gwynneth look at each other and smile like they have a secret. "Gwynneth and I got to decide what the money will be used for."

"Tell us," I say.

"You'll find out," Gwynneth says.

"No secrets!" Megan says.

"I'll tell you a secret right now," Vee says. "I told Gwynneth a lot of lies about all my great accomplishments—that I was a model, and a star athlete, and super popular."

"Those are lies?" Gwynneth asks.

"Yes," I say. I'm nervous. Will she hate me?

Gwynneth bends forward, laughing hard.

I'm happy she thinks it's so funny. "That's hysterical," she says. "I wanted you to think I was super cool. But I'm not cool at all!"

"You're not?" I say at the same time as Vee and Megan.

"No!" Gwynneth says. "I wanted you to think I was, but I'm not."

I like her better right away. "Thank goodness!" Megan says. "I never liked cool kids very much."

"That's so funny," Vee says.

"I'll tell you another secret about myself that no one knows," Gwynneth says. "I write fan fiction. I write episodes of *Vampire Diaries*."

"Too scary," Vee says with a shudder.

"I write fan fiction, too!" Megan shouts. "I write about *Lord of the Rings*."

"You never told us that!" I say. I turn to Vee. "Did you know that?" I ask.

"I didn't know that," Vee says. "Can we see it?"

Megan doesn't answer because she's talking intently to Gwynneth. I assume they're talking about fan fiction. I'm amazed. I guess we think we know the people closest to us but there's always more to find out.

I glance across the lobby and see Megan's parents talking to Mom and Vee's dad. Mom holds Vee's dad's hand!!!! OMG!!!!!!!!!!!!!!!!!!!!!!!!!!!!!!!!!!

I guess I saw it coming. How could I not? It's a good thing. It would be awesome if Vee and I became stepsisters. We'd have to make Megan an honorary stepsister. Maybe by then we'll even have to include Gwynneth in on the stepsister thing too. We'll see.

Vee sees Ethan and hurries over to him. He kisses her lightly on the cheek. Megan and I punch each other excitedly on the arms. It's just a cheek kiss, but still. They hold hands!

Megan and I stamp our feet with the thrill of it.

"Is that Vee's boyfriend?" Gwynneth asks us.

"It is now!" I reply

The concert starts. Gwynneth and Vee get to have the first two rows for themselves and their guests. We meet Gwynneth's closest friends, who are on her Mathletes team. Ethan and Vee sit together, still holding hands.

Heather May is there with her camerawoman. She approaches Gwynneth and Vee and has them step out into the aisle. "You did it, girls," she says as her camerawoman films.

"We sure did!" Vee says.

"This is my friend Olivia Howard," Gwynneth says. It's kind of dumb, but I have to give her cred for trying to make up for her past mistake.

There's an opening act of kids in a band called Free Spirits from Shoreham High. They're actually pretty good.

When they finish, the principals from the two schools get on stage. Mr. Hall, our principal, has a microphone. "We are so happy to see all you students from our two different schools here together in this terrific new performing arts center. We hope you talk and get to know each other. Because this contest has brought us together, Shoreham and Pleasant Hill districts will be sponsoring a lot more joint ventures like this. We're so grateful to Channel 14 for bringing our two school districts together in this way."

The crowd cheers wildly. Everyone is in such a great mood!

Mr. Hall continues once the cheers die down. "Our two winners have decided together how they want the money from concert ticket sales to be used. The Shoreham and Pleasant Hill school districts are going to invest in a mobile concussion awareness unit that will travel from school district to school district conducting concussion awareness seminars and giving out materials."

"Let's have our two winners come up on stage," says Ms. Jones, the Shoreham principal.

Everyone applauds. Gwynneth and Vee hurry onto the stage, where they shake hands, and then they hug. "Is there anything you would like to say to your friends in the audience?" Ms. Jones asks them.

"Just thanks for being here," Gwynneth says when she is handed the microphone.

Vee is never shy, so when it's her turn it's no surprise that she makes the most of it. "I'm so glad to have gotten to know Gwynneth Plotkin through this contest. She never gave up. I'd also like to thank my pals Lulu Vance and Megan Hardwick . . ."

Megan and I stand up and pump our fists. Everyone cheers for us. It's the best!

". . . and all the students at Pleasant Hill Middle who were so supportive in every way," Vee continues. "Enjoy the show, everybody!"

The audience goes crazy with cheering. Vee and Gwynneth wave as they move to the side of the stage and stand beside Ms. Jones.

Mr. Hall steps forward with the microphone. "And now put your hands together for Boys Being Dudes!"

The audience goes absolutely berserk as Boys Being

Dudes runs onto the stage. As they do, Derek, the lead singer, grabs hold of Vee's hand and leads her to the front of the stage. Josh, the bass guitarist, takes hold of Gwynneth's hand. "Give it up for Gwynneth and Vee!" Derek shouts into the microphone.

Megan and I shout until our throats hurt. It's deafening. Vee is smiling from ear to ear. Gwynneth is blushing bright red, but she also grins. I would faint if I was up there—just completely faint!

Gwynneth and Vee go back off to the side as BBD starts to play. They are so awesome! Even better in person than on their recording. It takes only seconds for everyone to be on their feet, totally into it. Derek is amazing. So dreamy. Everyone is so into the band.

Especially Megan. I see her wave to one of the band members. And then I see Joe, the drummer, waving back.

CHAPTER 26

So, BACK TO REALITY. The concert was a blast and a half, but now I'm back at school. Dad has decided that he'll drive the extra forty-five minutes to work and we'll stay right where we are. Yay! The fact that he doesn't want to move that far from Lulu's mom might have something to do with it, but he also wants Eric and me to be happy—which we are.

Gwynneth was sad to hear that I'm not coming to Shoreham after all, but she and I stay in touch. In fact—and this is really amazing—our Snapstreak is still going. That's right! We Snap at least once a day! Lulu and Megan Snap with her, too.

GQB2the2ndpwr

Queen of numbers! Mathletes rule!

Luloony

Megawatt

V-Ness

ABOUT THE AUTHOR

SUZANNE WEYN'S most recent young adult novel *Bionic* was published by Scholastic Press in October 2016. Her other well-known novels include the award-winning Bar Code Tattoo trilogy, the ecological thriller *Empty*, and *Reincarnation*, among many other published works. She currently teaches writing as an adjunct professor at Medgar Evers College, and at Westchester Community College. You can find her at suzanneweynbooks.com.

YOUR NOTES!

NOTES